My Border Collie World

Ruth Simerly

Copyright © 2016 Ruth Simerly
All rights reserved.

ISBN: 1539609928
ISBN 13: 9781539609926
Library of Congress Control Number: 2016917503
CreateSpace Independent Publishing Platform
North Charleston, South Carolina

CHAPTER 1

We Find Each Other

I REMEMBER THE first moment I saw Laura. I knew right away that Laura would be my person.

Our meeting took place at a small-town veterinary clinic that also served as the local animal shelter. The first time Laura saw me, I was filthy from months of running through mud and manure and gravel, trying to get away from people and dogs that chased me.

One of my back legs hurt most of the time. It was injured when I was thrown from the back of a pickup truck as the driver turned a corner too fast. I had been riding in the truck with some other dogs. We were not restrained in any way. We were returning from an afternoon of training.

I was part of a litter of border collie puppies being raised to herd sheep and to participate in herding competitions at fairs, rodeos, and similar events. Training was easy. It wasn't difficult to outsmart sheep. I was fed well and seldom scolded, but as one of several ranch dogs, I didn't have my own person.

After I was thrown from the truck on that fateful day, I was dazed and could barely walk. I hurt all over, but I ignored my pain and desperately started running in the direction the truck was traveling. I couldn't catch it. No one inside the truck saw my fall. I watched as the truck disappeared from view. I never saw it again.

I knew we had traveled a long way from the ranch. I wondered how I would get back home. It was late March, so the weather wasn't a big problem.

For weeks, I wandered up and down roads, canal banks, and paths, trying to find someone I knew. All I found were angry, vicious dogs and people who chased me away. I was hungry most of the time and ate only animals that had been killed by cars or by other animals. Once in a while, I would find another dog's bowl in a yard and finish what was left before someone chased me away.

Spring ended, and summer arrived. I searched for water as well as food. I often wanted to jump into water to keep cool and quench my thirst. Some of the water was so dirty that it was almost mud. I thought of all the times I had herded sheep, how I always tried to do a good job. I wondered if I'd ever guide another sheep.

Summer passed. I survived fall and winter. Some days, I questioned whether I would freeze or starve first, but I had a strong desire to live.

Spring finally arrived. I appreciated the warmth, sunshine, and longer days of the season. One afternoon, I limped slowly along a dirt road in the country. My feet were sore. I was filthy. My stomach was so empty that I wondered if it would ever hold food again. A car approached me from behind, and I hurried off the road. I'd learned how to avoid being hit by cars or things people threw at me from car windows.

The car slowed ahead of me and stopped. A middle-aged woman stepped out of the vehicle. I started to run, but she called quietly to me and walked slowly toward me. I sensed she wouldn't hurt me. I crept forward. She offered a piece of sandwich to me. I was so hungry that I almost snapped it out of her hand. She took a small rope from her jeans pocket and placed it around my neck while speaking softly to me. I didn't resist. She led me slowly toward her car. Hers was the first kindness I had experienced in a long time. I trusted her. As dirty and smelly as I was, she opened the back door of her car and motioned for me to get inside and sit on the floor. I followed her directions, although I was unsure and tucked my tail between my legs. The woman climbed into the driver's seat.

Before she started the car, the woman reached into a plastic bag and drew out half of a sandwich. She carefully handed it over the seat to me. I gobbled every bite. When I finished, we drove away. I hunched down on the floor next to the back seat of the car.

During our drive into a town, the woman talked quietly to me. We stopped at a large building set back from the road. It was the veterinary clinic and animal shelter.

The woman climbed out of her car and went inside the building. A few minutes later, she and another woman returned to the car. The other woman carried a long leash. She spoke to me and gently placed the leash around my neck. Both women talked to and about me. I heard them say I looked like I was about a year old and appeared to be a border collie or cattle dog. The two women walked me into the building and led me into to one of the dog runs.

The run was about four feet wide and six feet long—enough space for one dog. I saw a blanket in one corner. The women brought me fresh water and food. I hadn't seen so much food in many months. I tried not to gobble, but I was hungry. The women's smiles gave me encouragement. After I ate every bit of food, I lay down on the blanket and fell asleep, feeling safer than I had in a long time.

I saw three other dogs. Two of them barked when I entered. They stopped barking when the women left, and they ignored me. Two of them were in much better shape than I was, although an older dog looked as if his owner had treated him badly. I saw hairless patches on his hide and a nasty cut on one of his hips. He seemed to be happy to be at the shelter and wagged his tail when the women approached.

The next morning, I was fed again and led outside to do my business. When I returned to my run, I heard the voice of the woman who first let me into the building. My rescuer called her Trudy. Trudy was talking to another woman at the reception desk. The visitor asked about a dog who belonged to her friend. The dog has escaped from its yard, and the owner was worried. Trudy told her she didn't have a dog in the shelter like the one described. That night Laura called her friend and was relieved to learn that the dog had found its way home,

Trudy asked the visitor if she had found another companion since her dog died. The woman said it had been about seven months and she didn't feel ready for another pet. A few days later Laura told me about losing her dog, Target. I felt sad about her dog's passing, but glad that Laura and I had found each other.

I was surprised when Trudy came to my run and took me into the reception area. I didn't know Trudy was searching for a home for me so soon. I saw Laura for the first time. For me, it was love at first sight. Laura wore jeans and boots, and her hair was pulled into a ponytail. It took me about ten seconds to decide that Laura was the person for me.

My own person! I struggled against the leash in my eagerness to bolt across the room. I snuggled up to Laura to let her know that she was the most wonderful person I had ever seen. I always wanted my own person and hoped it would be someone just like Laura.

Laura backed away from me quickly and even a little fearfully. I guess I came on a little strong. I was dirty and smelly and obviously without manners.

"Oh, Laura," Trudy exclaimed, "he loves you already. He would make such a great companion. Dr. Atkins examined him early this morning and said he's only about a year old."

Laura glanced at me, practically wrapped around her feet.

I must have been quite a sight—skin and bones, covered with mud and manure, and favoring my back leg.

Laura shook her head, but Trudy didn't give up.

"Why not take him for a week? No commitment. See how you get along with him. You should have another dog. I know how much you cared for Target."

I scooted up on my haunches, waved my paw in the air, and dropped it when Laura told me to do so.

"You mean I could take him temporarily, like on trial? I never knew the shelter did that."

"Yes, you can. He's a special dog. We'll never know if he has papers, but he certainly is all border collie. They are such an intelligent breed. And he really likes you."

I crept over to Laura's feet again and lay there.

Laura didn't hesitate this time. "OK. At least for a week. He certainly is filthy. I'll take him to the dog wash before we go home. I'll see how much I can scrub off of him. Then I'll have to clean out my truck."

"So what are you naming him?"

"He doesn't have a name?"

"No. As you can see, he's a stray and arrived only late yesterday. I need a name to put on his papers."

"Trudy, I can't think of a name. I'm drawing a blank." Laura gazed at me. "Oh, wait a minute. How about Shep?"

Laura said "Shep" again. I perked up my ears, wagged my tail, and waved a paw, letting her know the name was OK with me.

I walked close to Laura as we left the shelter together. We stopped at a small black pickup truck. I hesitated, not wanting to jump into another truck bed. Laura guided me to the passenger side of the cab and told me I would be riding next to her. She opened the door, searched behind the seat, and spread out a large towel. She motioned for me to jump in. I, of course, made a flying leap onto the seat. I was ready to go.

As our truck pulled away from the shelter, I didn't know where we were going, but I didn't care. We drove through the small town and parked at a pet store on the outskirts.

Laura placed a rope leash around my neck and guided me from the truck right into the store. She asked the sales clerk if the dog wash was in use. The clerk waved us toward the back of the building. Laura led me to a room with a tub, a sink, and all kinds of bottles and hoses.

I had never seen a dog bathtub before. Laura encouraged me to get in, and, carefully, I did. She took a hose with a sprayer, turned on the water, and washed the mud and manure from my coat. I didn't protest. It actually felt good. She even used shampoo. I think she was pleased with her effort when she finally finished. As she rubbed me down with towels, she kept saying that I was a beautiful dog. She seemed amazed at what a little water and dog shampoo could do. A few minutes with a blow-dryer finished my first bathing experience.

Laura paid for my bath and also for a couple of bowls, some dog food, and a collar and leash. The store owner greeted Laura as we left and said I was a handsome dog. I smiled at him and wagged my tail.

Again, I didn't know where we were going when Laura started the truck. We drove away from the dog wash a short distance out of town to a mobile-home park.

Laura turned her truck into one of the larger units with a fenced yard. She helped me out of the truck and led me into the yard. I immediately sniffed all over the place. Laura watched me as she unloaded the truck.

Laura called, "Shep," and I ran to her. We sat on the steps together. I placed my head on her lap. She stroked my face and then hugged me. I knew I had my forever home.

Laura took me back to the shelter but only to complete the rest of the paperwork to adopt me. She asked Dr. Atkins about my injured leg. The veterinarian told her I had a bad bruise on my left hind leg that hadn't had a chance to properly heal.

Dr. Atkins also told Laura that she was lucky to have me. He said that border collies were loyal companions and were intelligent and protective. He told her that border collies were working farm dogs, originally from Scotland and England, and were thought by experts to be the best sheepherding dogs in the world. He said that I was about the average height of twenty inches, and although thin now, I would probably eventually weigh about forty pounds. Although I was scrawny and didn't look my best, we border collies were handsome dogs. My black-and-white coloring was the most familiar, but border collies also came in colors like brown, bluish gray, and brown or rust, and they frequently had white markings.

Dr. Atkins cautioned Laura that I needed lots of exercise to be contented and maybe a job to do, like catching Frisbees. Laura told Dr. Atkins that she had a large yard and access to other areas where I could run and play with Frisbees.

When we were finished with the vet and paperwork, I went home a happy dog.

CHAPTER 2

The Rest of the Family

LAURA LIVED ALONE in a three-bedroom home. She had turned one bedroom into her office. Laura worked as a writer at home most of the time. She told me not to bother her when she was at her computer, which was fine with me. We still had plenty of time together. After all, the two of us were a family.

I prefer being outdoors, so I usually stayed in the yard when Laura was at her computer. I always moved into the house when it began to get dark and often spent the night sleeping near the front door. I was Laura's watchdog during the night and guarded her home until morning, although there wasn't much around to put her in danger.

Laura's sister, nephew, and niece visited her often. She also had many friends, both male and female. Laura enjoyed the outdoors. She played tennis in the summer and enjoyed cross-country skiing and snowshoeing in the winter.

I was particularly fond of the dinners Laura prepared for her family and her friends. There always seemed to be something left over for me. The only other times Laura let me have table scraps was after she went out for a meal. She usually brought me back a treat.

The first time Laura's niece and nephew came, I ran to a corner of the yard. I remembered the kids who chased me and threw sticks and rocks at me.

Laura came out of the house and walked over to me. She asked Brad and Connie to move quietly behind her. Laura petted me and assured me that Brad and Connie meant no harm. They wanted to get to know me. She motioned for the two kids to step around her and pet me. I trembled for a moment, but the kids spoke so kindly and stroked me so gently that I decided they must be all right, especially after Brad picked up a Frisbee and threw it down the yard for me.

I ran after the Frisbee, caught it midair, and carried it back to drop at Brad's feet. I don't bring a Frisbee back to the hands of the thrower. After all, I am not a retriever. I am a herder. I expect people to pick up my Frisbee and throw it again.

Laura's sister, Marj, the mother of Brad and Connie, did not like dogs. In fact, I don't think she liked much of anything. She was so different from Laura. Brad and Connie, on the other hand, were more like Laura. Once I got to know them, I thought they were great. Connie also could throw a Frisbee.

I didn't see a man with Marj, Connie, and Brad. Maybe that was why Marj was so unhappy. Laura explained the situation after dinner one night when she and I were alone. Marj's husband left them for a woman he had met while traveling for his job. Marj was bitter. It all started a couple of years ago. The next time Marj came over, I tried to give her more attention, but she pushed me away. I felt sorry for her.

Laura and Marj had a brother, Duane, who also visited. He sometimes wore a military uniform and was a US Air Force pilot stationed in a nearby state. I met him when he came to town to do special training with the national guard.

Duane loved dogs and missed the one at home with his family.

The happiest I saw Marj in the early days was one Sunday when she, Brad, and Connie had dinner with Duane at our home.

Laura had one more family member I met soon after she and I got together—her father. He was the first person I ever saw in a wheelchair. I soon realized he couldn't walk. When I met him, I ran over and put my head near his knees as the wheelchair stopped. He hadn't invited me over, but he immediately reached down and petted me.

"Hi, fella," he told me as he continued to stroke me. "I'm glad Laura found you."

I wagged my tail.

Laura knelt beside me. "Dad, we found each other at the animal shelter. You should have seen him the first time I did. He was mud and manure from nose to tip of tail."

I remembered that day. I had splashed through a muddy cattle feedlot, chased by two dogs.

Laura's father laughed. "He's certainly a fine-looking dog now."

I wagged my tail in agreement. I had already gained more than five pounds, and Laura had brushed my coat that morning.

I wondered about Laura's mother until one day I heard her father talking about the woman. He said he hadn't heard from her for several years. He asked Laura if she had been in contact with her.

"Dad," Laura replied, "I don't think Mother would ever get in touch with me. You and I are much too close. She may let Marj know where she is sometimes, but Marj has not said anything to me."

Laura's father shrugged. "It's probably best that we don't know."

"I was so angry when Mother left you right after the accident, even before she knew you'd be in a wheelchair. I'm thankful I was an adult and didn't have to live with her."

"You know, Laura," her father said, "this wheelchair has actually been a positive life change, in a way. I've done things I never would have done before, traveled to places I thought I never had time to see, and worked to develop things to make life easier for the rest of us who don't get around so well anymore. I'd certainly rather have the use of my legs again, but I've found out how to enjoy life the way it is."

I was lying beside Laura's father during this conversation, so I sat up and placed my head on his ankles. He reached down and stroked me.

"Shep seems to know what I'm saying."

"Maybe because of his chronic leg problem," Laura said.

Laura's mother was not mentioned again for many months. When her name came up, it was because she had been killed. A drunk driver slammed into her car. She died instantly.

The family gathered at Laura's home after her mother's funeral service. Laura prepared a meal.

It was a quiet afternoon. I moved from one person to another, and almost everyone took time to acknowledge me. I even approached Marj, but she shooed me away. I vowed to keep trying.

Later that afternoon, a strange man came to the door. I barked. Laura motioned for me to be quiet, and I was. The man moved into the living room, and the family greeted him. Several of the men shook hands with him. Laura greeted him with a hug. I moved closer to Marj, not too close, to hear her comment.

"I certainly didn't expect him to be here. I don't think he's seen Laura for years, and she's the only one who knew him at all."

Laura's brother whispered to Marj. "Even if the engagement didn't work out, Laura and Adam have remained friends. I'm glad he came."

Duane greeted Adam.

I was curious. Several men had visited our home since I arrived. Laura prepared dinner for some of them, or they went out for dinner or somewhere else together. I didn't sense that she cared much for any of them. Maybe Adam was the reason.

Sometimes I wonder what happened to my dog family. I was one in a litter of five, but I never spent much time with any of them. As soon as I was weaned, I was taken away to begin life as a working dog. Maybe all dogs leave their families when they are young. It would have been nice to know my dog family, but I remembered how lucky I was. I had my own family. I had Laura.

CHAPTER 3

Camp Not So Heavenly

LAURA AND I were spending a few quiet weeks during the summer. Then one Friday afternoon, as I lay stretched out on my favorite rug in the kitchen, the telephone rang. Laura answered the phone in her office, so I didn't hear the first part of the conversation. My curiosity overcame my desire to relax, so I hurried into the office. Laura had some interesting phone conversations, and this turned out to be one of them.

As soon as she hung up the phone, Laura moved into her bedroom and dragged out her duffel bag from underneath her bed.

I knew then that she would be leaving for more than a few hours. The duffel bag meant she would be wearing outdoor clothes.

Laura noticed me standing at the door.

"Oh, Shep, I forgot about you."

Laura dropped the duffel bag and picked up a phone. She called the Barkley Boarding Kennels, where I would stay when Laura was out of town. As she talked, she became stressed.

"You're sure you're booked up over the holiday weekend? Do you know anywhere else I might board Shep for a week?"

No one at the kennel had any suggestions for Laura. She put the phone down slowly, and then she picked it up and dialed another number. I listened as she explained that she couldn't find a kennel for me and couldn't go to church camp.

Laura listened for a few minutes, and then her voice sounded excited.

"You're sure it's all right? Super!"

Laura finished packing her duffel bag, hurried out to the kitchen entrance, and returned with my backpack. I need almost as many travel items as Laura does.

She stopped and spoke to me. "Shep, you're coming with me to help out at church camp. One of the counselors can't go, and Pastor Jim just found out a short time ago. We'll be working with twelve-year-old girls."

Laura packed my favorite rug, food, two dishes, treats, a long lightweight chain, and my Frisbee.

Less than an hour after Laura received the phone call, she had packed camp stuff for both of us, checked the inside and outside of the house, let me outside a couple of times, and thrown our travel bags into the back of the truck. She changed into jeans and a sweatshirt, locked the doors, and called me to come with her to the truck.

I quickly jumped into my usual place, on the front seat next to Laura. She wouldn't allow me to ride in the truck bed because she knew how dangerous it could be. Sometimes she would speak angrily to people who placed their animals in the back of a pickup without restraining them. Her voice was louder than usual during these conversations.

Once in a while, I remembered it was a truck bed that brought Laura and me together all those months ago. I was grateful to have this home and that Laura had me. We didn't have a large, fancy house, but she gave me food, treats, and Frisbees and, more importantly, kept me with her whenever she could.

Laura worked at home on her computer or phone. I knew I had more attention from my person than most other dogs did.

We drove to Laura's church parking lot, which was empty except for Pastor Jim standing beside his car.

Pastor Jim hurried over to greet us. He lifted all of our travel gear from the truck bed and put it into the trunk of his car.

Laura called me over to Pastor Jim's car and opened the back door for me.

This smelled like an adventure.

As we drove out of the parking lot, Pastor Jim told Laura how grateful he was that she had agreed to be a last-minute substitute counselor. Otherwise, he would have had to cancel the camp for the girls.

I curled up on the back seat and went to sleep. I would often sleep when traveling with Laura, especially if I'd seen the area before. Laura would wake me when we arrived at our destination.

I felt stiff when I woke up, so I knew we had traveled quite a distance. We stopped at a country store. Laura spoke to me, snapped on my leash, and led me to a field where I took care of my needs. She led me back to the car and filled my water dish.

We were soon on the road again and into the mountains. I sat up and looked around. I had never been there before. We arrived at a small town and drove past a large sign, "Camp Heavenly," with an arrow pointing to the right. We turned at the sign and approached a log lodge surrounded by cabins.

Pastor Jim parked the car and went inside the lodge. Laura and I waited in the car. When Pastor Jim returned, he spoke with Laura and pointed up a hill next to the lodge.

Laura climbed out of the car and opened the back door for me to join her. She snapped my leash onto my collar. We climbed the slight hill to a cabin near the top. When we entered the cabin, I counted eleven beds in a cramped room. The beds were small, except for one bed in the corner, which was considerably larger. Laura tossed her duffel bag and my backpack onto that bed. So Laura and I were going to sleep in this room. But why all those other beds? Surely no one had planned for all those beds to be used in that tiny room. Maybe it meant I could have my choice of beds or try a different one every night.

Pastor Jim called for us. Laura kept me on my leash—an embarrassment to me. I thought it must be camp rules. Laura certainly knew I would behave in this strange place.

Laura and I hurried down to Pastor Jim. He informed Laura that the campers would be arriving at any moment and that he and Laura needed to set up the registration table.

People soon began arriving with suitcases and duffel bags. Not adult people—half-size. The boys and girls reminded me of students I saw at the middle school back home. I was uneasy and even barked a time or two. Laura immediately scolded me.

When I was homeless, two boys on bicycles tried to run me down. With my injured leg, I couldn't escape. I don't know what would have happened if a kind man hadn't chased the boys away from me.

When the camp registration was finished, we had a total of ten girls and five boys in our group. Pastor Jim and his assistant, Luke, were responsible for the five boys, and Laura and I had ten girls in our care. Pastor Jim was also in charge of the camp.

When the girls were introduced, several of them told Laura she was too old to be their counselor. They snickered and giggled as Laura tried to gather all the information from them that she needed. If I were alone with them, I would have taught them some manners. Laura laughed off the unkind remarks, but I knew they bothered her.

As we finished the registration, I nudged Laura. She reached down and petted me. Together, we could handle these rude girls for a week. No wonder their parents or grandparents sent them away to camp.

I wondered if it was fair for Laura to have ten girls alone and for Pastor Jim and Luke to have only five boys with the two of them.

But Laura had me.

Laura and I accompanied the girls to the cabin to help them get settled. The campers were all shapes and sizes. It seemed to me that they brought more makeup than clothes, and eight of them weren't even teenagers yet. Two of the teenagers shouldn't have been in the group, but Pastor Jim allowed them to stay. He muttered something about a break for the family.

While she was helping the girls, Laura left me outside the cabin. She fastened me to a tree with the chain so I could have as much freedom as possible. She put out water and food. I drank the water, but I was too excited to eat.

After all the girls were settled in the cabin, Laura took them to the lodge for the evening meal. She strolled back alone from dinner and sat on the top step of the cabin entrance. I hopped up beside her, and she hugged me. I could tell she was upset.

"Oh, Shep," she cried as she buried her face into my coat. "Those girls are impossible. I walked over to sit down at their table, and they all got up and moved. I sat alone until the kitchen crew came in and sat with me."

The girls moved away from Laura again at breakfast. That was the last time she stayed to eat in the dining room. She ate in the kitchen or brought food and shared it with me. I was so pleased I was with Laura.

All the campers had an hour of free time each day. Free time meant the campers had no assigned activities during that time and could hang out in and around the lodge. Jim and the lodge workers supervised the campers. Pastor Jim said that Laura and I could leave the camp and explore. The first day, Laura and I walked into the village about a half mile away. Laura bought some snacks, and we shared a beef sandwich at an outside café. What a pleasant break from the camp. Free time was my favorite hour of the day that entire week.

Laura was responsible for the care of the cabin as well as the girls. The campers ignored her efforts to get them to do their share. They trashed the place almost every day. Laura appealed to Pastor Jim, but he was no help. He thought the campers should have fun and freedom, even if the fun was at the expense of the adults.

I thought Laura would have gone home the second night if we had our truck. The counselor who decided not to come was smart. She must have known the girls who would be at camp.

One night, Laura had a difficult time settling the girls for the night. The campers had been told "lights out" at ten o'clock. "Lights out" to them meant "flashlights on," and the girls continued with their mischief.

Laura waited a few minutes and snapped on the cabin lights.

"OK, girls," she yelled. "I've had enough. Give me your flashlights now, or I'll take them from you."

I growled, surprising Laura and the girls, but she didn't scold me. Everyone in that cabin knew we meant business. Laura gathered the flashlights into a pillowcase.

I hardly heard a sound for the rest of the night.

The next morning, the girls as a group complained to Pastor Jim about the flashlights. They convinced Pastor Jim that they couldn't find their way to the bath and restroom building at night without them. Pastor Jim rescued the flashlights for the girls, but he did warn them to heed the ten o'clock rule for the rest of the week. The girls ignored the warning.

Ruth Simerly

Laura decided that if it was light the girls wanted, it was light they would get. She left all of the cabin lights on all night, every night for the rest of the week. The girls tried to keep their heads covered to avoid the constant light. Light didn't bother me. Light didn't bother Laura. I had seen her fall asleep on her couch or in her chair with all the lights on. The girls complained loudly, but not one approached Pastor Jim.

The boys in the camp surprised me. I backed away from them and barked the first time they approached. I remembered the teasing and taunting from the likes of them. I found out that at least one of the boys, Ken, had a dog back home. One afternoon when we were all outside the lodge, I carried my Frisbee over to Ken. He asked me if I wanted him to throw it. I jumped and barked and ran up to and away from him. He smiled and threw my Frisbee. I ran after it and caught it on the run. The other boys cheered, and I had Frisbee pals for the rest of the week.

The girls even joined in the Frisbee play. I suspected they were trying to get the boys' attention.

The most frightening experience for Laura happened on the day of a hike. The hike was long, especially for Laura and me since we were sent in the wrong direction by one of the girls who chose to stay behind. Pastor Jim let her stay at the lodge. She had twisted her ankle coming from the cabin to breakfast that morning and insisted she couldn't walk that far. The kitchen leader agreed to supervise her inside the lodge.

We finally caught up with the group and finished the hike with them. I enjoyed playing with the boys on the trail and even chased my Frisbee down the mountain once in a while.

After we returned to the lodge late in the afternoon, one of the girls, Deb, discovered that she had left her camera on a rock where the group took a lunch break. Deb cried because the camera had special meaning for her. Her father, who no longer lived with Deb and her mother, had given Deb the camera before he left. Deb became almost hysterical as the afternoon faded.

Laura volunteered to go back with Deb to look for the camera. It was early evening, and I knew it would be dark soon. I trotted over to go with Laura and Deb, but Pastor Jim caught my collar and made me stay behind. I struggled against his hand until Laura assured me it would be OK for me to stay behind. I guess Pastor Jim thought I would attract a wild animal or go chase one. I was not a happy dog.

I watched from the edge of the lawn and glared at Pastor Jim as Deb ran ahead of Laura down the road toward the hiking trail.

Deb stayed so far ahead that Laura lost sight of her at times. The trail wove around boulders and trees. Deb suddenly disappeared around a large boulder. Laura shouted for Deb and whistled into the forest. No sound returned to Laura. Laura searched around the area, moving in every direction from the boulder. Deb had simply disappeared. Laura fought off visions of Deb being snatched from the trail or falling into the rushing river only a few yards from the path.

As it grew darker, Laura headed back toward the lodge to bring additional searchers to cover more of the mountain. Laura trotted down the mountain and continued to yell for Deb as she hurried down the trail.

Near the foot of the mountain, Laura paused. She thought she heard a faint response to her shouting. She stopped. Deb was calling her name. Guided by Deb's voice, Laura moved off the trail and found Deb propped against a tree. The girl had taken a wrong turn, slid down the mountain, and injured her leg. Deb was screaming, but her voice didn't carry far, especially against the roar of the river. Deb couldn't see Laura, and Laura couldn't see Deb. Deb was lucky that Laura arrived where she could hear Deb's screams.

Laura stood above Deb. She was angry but also relieved to have found Deb. The girl tried to stand on her injured leg and cried out in pain. Deb remained standing despite the pain and begged Laura to help her search for the camera. Laura agreed to a quick search of the lunch area, even though the sun had set. Laura reached into her pocket for her flashlight, and Deb retrieved hers.

Deb never complained about her leg as they combed the area where the group had stopped. Deb focused her flashlight at the place on the rock where she had lunch.

"Laura, Laura. I found it. Here at the base of this rock!"

Laura sighed with relief. Deb hugged Laura and quickly stepped away from her. The two of them started down the trail to the lodge.

I paced along the edge of the lodge lawn for most of the time that Laura and Deb were gone. I saw them before they saw me, and I rushed out to meet Laura. It was dark beyond the lawn. I glared at Deb and turned away from her and Pastor Jim. The other girls gathered around Deb. Laura, of course, told me the whole story. What irritated me most was that Deb never said thank you to Laura.

Although Laura and I had to deal with the problems created by the girls, we still had some fun. During one of our free hours, we explored a meadow near the lodge. I almost ran into a deer. We both were sniffing along the ground and didn't see each other until it was nearly too late. Deer living around the lodge were tame. I was impressed by their beauty. I didn't even consider chasing them, although I thought it might be fun to herd the deer. I didn't get the chance.

I enjoyed the campfires at night when everyone gathered to sing, toast marshmallows, and eat something called s'mores. Neither marshmallows nor s'mores appealed to me.

I also looked forward to the daily morning hike up a nearby hill to a large wooden cross for worship service. In fact, I liked everything about the church camp but the girl campers.

Laura had another unpleasant experience when Pastor Jim asked her to judge items found during a camp scavenger hunt. The campers were divided into teams. Five of the girls were on one team and five on another. Pastor Jim said the winner of the scavenger hunt would be the team that found the biggest, smallest, prettiest, or some other specific feature. Laura was asked to check out everything and declare the winner in each category. Since the girls were in two teams, one team would always win and be pleased and the other would lose and be disgusted with Laura. She couldn't win. I was delighted when the grand prize went to the boys' team.

The night before the week was finished, Pastor Jim held a talent contest—boys against girls. The boys included me in their talent, which was a Frisbee game. The boys stood in a circle and tossed my Frisbee back and forth, throwing it toward me every other time as I moved around the circle. The boys and I performed flawlessly and won the contest. I received hugs from the boys and even from some of the girls. I believe the girls used me to get closer to the boys.

The next morning, the sight of the girls packing their duffel bags and suitcases kept my tail wagging. I trotted down to meet the parents, or whoever arrived to pick up the girls. I wanted to be sure all of the girls were going home.

Several adults hugged Laura and thanked her for being a counselor. They seemed particularly grateful that Laura had been the person staying with the girls. Parents and other adults are smarter than their kids or grandkids.

Later that afternoon, I waited impatiently for my backpack to be put into the trunk of Pastor Jim's car. I never left the parking area; I paced back and forth near the car's back door.

When Pastor Jim finally came out and signaled for me to get into the car, I leaped right onto the back seat. I lay down and waited for Pastor Jim and Laura. I was ready to leave Camp Heavenly.

I didn't even want to stop for a stretch on the way home, but I jumped out for a few minutes when Laura insisted.

I was always thrilled to get home from the boarding kennel, but I couldn't remember being so happy to see my yard as I was when we returned from Camp Heavenly.

CHAPTER 4

Danger on Ice

ONE OF THE things I loved most about being in Laura's family was sharing a desire to be outdoors as often as possible.

A special destination was land owned by one of Laura's friends.

Laura had a key to the gate to access the area, and we could go there whenever we wanted.

This special place was called Grey Wings and consisted of about forty acres. The entire area was fenced along the county road, so I was allowed to run free. A river bordered the land on the other side.

Grey Wings was the right name for the property. Hundreds of Canada geese nested and raised their young every year within its boundaries. Several fishponds had been constructed. Laura and her friends often fed the bluegill, carp, and trout in these ponds. Water diverted from the river filled the ponds and then was channeled back into the river.

I was allowed to go to Grey Wings year-round because I never bothered the nesting geese or their goslings. The idea of herding all the geese occasionally crossed my mind, but I realized I probably couldn't get away with such antics.

During our first trip to Grey Wings, I was skeptical about all that water, even though most border collies love to swim. Large bodies of water were not appealing when I was a stray. The first day I visited Grey Wings, I jumped into a pond and enjoyed swimming.

Laura took me to the river. She warned me that if I jumped into the fast-moving water, then I might get swept away and she couldn't save me. I watched the rushing water, and I agreed with her. After that first visit, Laura and I knew Grey Wings would be one of our favorite playgrounds.

About the time Laura learned of my love for water, she also learned that Frisbees would become my favorite toys.

I don't know how I decided I liked Frisbees. Maybe it just came from being a border collie. The first time Laura threw a new Frisbee to me, I chased it and caught it in midair. I caught most of the Frisbees thrown to me if they were anywhere near the spot where I was running or standing.

The ponds at Grey Wings were perfect for our Frisbee-catching outings. Laura was careful about throwing the Frisbee on land and avoided throwing it into a pond. One day, however, the wind caught the Frisbee and sent it sailing into a pond.

I stared at my Frisbee from the bank and barked.

Laura hurried to her truck and brought back a rake. She recovered my Frisbee. About a week later, a Frisbee accidentally flew into the pond again. This time, Laura had nothing to use to retrieve it.

I wasn't concerned. I knew about the ponds now. I jumped into the water, swam out to the Frisbee, clamped it between my teeth, and swam to the shore, with Laura waving and cheering me on.

We didn't worry about Frisbees going into a pond after that, but we did lose a few when they landed on the edge of the pond and sank immediately.

I was allowed to rescue my Frisbees in the ponds, but Laura insisted that if one went into the river, it was gone. One day, the Frisbee landed in the river. Laura rushed to stand beside me, assuring me that the Frisbee was gone forever.

I stood on the bank for as long as Laura would allow. I then barked once at my lost Frisbee and followed Laura back to our truck. I'd like to think that somewhere the Frisbee drifted ashore and a dog or other animal retrieved it.

That fall brought strange weather. It turned so cold in November that the ponds began to freeze. One day at Grey Wings, my Frisbee skipped into a pond that had partially frozen over. I was eager to retrieve it. I gingerly tested the ice at the edge of the pond with one of my paws. Laura stood beside me almost immediately and shouted that I should move away from the edge because the ice was dangerous. I backed away.

Laura kept a close eye on me the rest of the time we were there, making certain I didn't sneak into the pond. I trotted around the edge, hoping that somehow the Frisbee would float over to me, but it stayed on a shelf of ice in the middle of the pond. I kept one eye on the Frisbee even as we drove away from Grey Wings. I didn't like going home without my Frisbee.

A few days later, we drove out to Grey Wings again. The temperature had stayed below freezing. When we stopped near the place where I'd lost my Frisbee, I jumped out of the truck and ran to the edge of the pond. I saw my Frisbee on the ice.

Before Laura could grab me, I leaped onto the ice. I heard the ice crack beneath my paws and was scared. I turned and carefully headed back toward the edge of the pond.

Laura stood on the bank. Her voice shook as she urged me to move close enough to the shore for her to grab me. I stood where I was. Laura yelled at me, insisting that my Frisbee had frozen into the pond. Even if I reached it, I wouldn't be able to remove it from the ice. I didn't listen.

I gathered my courage and trotted across the ice again, ignoring the cracking beneath my paws, gradually moving closer to my Frisbee.

After a few minutes, I stood above my Frisbee. I placed my front paw on the Frisbee's edge, expecting to flip it up and catch it as I did on land. Nothing happened. It was frozen into the ice. I struggled for a few minutes, but it did not budge.

I watched Laura desperately waving her arms at me. I tried again. I scratched at the Frisbee. I licked the ice that was holding it. I threw my weight against it.

On the bank, Laura began to unlace her boots. She thought she would have to rescue me. I pawed and licked until I couldn't do either anymore. Then the Frisbee moved slightly. I clamped my teeth on the Frisbee and yanked, and the ice released it. I trotted across the ice with my frozen Frisbee in my mouth.

Laura clapped and cheered, even though I knew she was angry, but she didn't reach for her boots. She must have known the ice wouldn't hold me until I could get to shore.

The ice cracked loudly beneath my paws as I neared the edge of the pond and suddenly gave way a few yards from the shore. I fell into the water.

Laura jumped into the icy pond as I floundered around in water that was deeper than I was tall. She caught me firmly around the body, planted her feet on the bank of the pond, and dragged and pushed me to the shore. She was soaking wet and shivering as she struggled to her feet.

I dropped my Frisbee, climbed up her front, and began licking her face. She moved away and ran to the truck, where she grabbed blankets and tried to dry us off. She started the truck and turned on the heater. After she had dried us off as well as she could, she motioned for me to get into the truck.

We drove home fast. Laura was out of her clothes before she was all the way into the house.

That evening, as Laura and I lay in front of her wood-burning fireplace, I suddenly remembered that I had not picked up my Frisbee from the bank. I'd left it behind. The Frisbee didn't seem important anymore.

CHAPTER 5

A Special Christmas Visit

SNOW HAD FALLEN during most of a December night. When Laura let me outside early the next morning, I stepped right into the snow—about four inches of it. I gingerly trotted over the lawn and saw that the snow was still falling. I remembered how cold I was when it snowed on me as a stray.

I lifted my head and blinked as the snowflakes landed close to my eyes. I snapped at the flakes as they drifted and caught a few in my mouth. Since I was out here, I might as well play in the snow—at least until Laura had my food ready. She always had a bowl of food and fresh water waiting for me in the morning. I didn't always eat it all until midafternoon, but I really liked knowing that food was available when I wanted to eat.

During December, our home was decorated with wreaths and angels and similar items. We didn't have a Christmas tree. Maybe Laura was concerned that I might accidentally knock it over. A neighboring beagle from across the back fence told me that December was the Christmas season—the time Christians celebrate the birth of Christ.

Laura went to church almost every Sunday and sometimes did other work there during the week. I learned a little about Christmas while watching Laura study her Bible and while she read its stories aloud.

During the Christmas season, people seemed to be nicer to one another than during any other time of the year. They gave gifts and cards and hugs. Laura baked cookies and made fudge, both of which were no-nos for me.

I didn't like sweet stuff anyway, with the important exception of ice cream.

On this December morning, I grew tired of romping in the snow. I hurried back into the house and shook my body on the entry rug. Laura rushed over with a towel and a hug. I felt warm all over.

My Border Collie World

Laura was dressed in a red sweater with a reindeer decoration and was wearing her boots. She tied tiny Christmas bells onto my collar and put a red bandanna around my neck. She told me we were going to a nursing home. She said that friends of a patient knew about me, and I should be proud of myself because few dogs were allowed in the nursing home. Her friend had asked that I visit the nursing home to bring cheer to the people living there. I had no idea what a nursing home was or what was expected of me. Another adventure?

A few minutes later, Laura snapped on my leash. She buckled me into my special harness and put a large plastic storage container in the bed of the truck.

We drove through town and onto a country road. I was relieved that Laura had placed heavy sandbags in the back of the truck. The weight of the sandbags kept the truck from sliding on the snow-covered road.

Laura parked in the driveway of a long one-story building. She told me to stay quiet while she went into the building to be sure we were both welcome visitors.

Laura removed the storage box from the bed of the truck and carried it into the building before returning for me. I had never been in a building this large. Laura gently urged me forward and tugged on my leash when I didn't move. She meant business, and I obediently trotted at her side.

Laura spoke to a woman at the door. "Bev, this is Shep. I'm sure the patients will enjoy his visit. He loves people and is a very gentle dog."

I thought the woman should have known that I was friendly by the way I was wagging my tail and stretching out my paw to greet her.

Laura opened the storage box, took out a large red bow, and secured it to my bandanna. I shook my head and heard the ringing bells on my collar. Now I wasn't so happy.

I thought it was quite enough to expect a self-respecting dog to wear a collar, especially one with Laura's name and phone number engraved on it. Didn't Laura know that if I was ever stolen or lost, I could find my way home by myself? I had found her, hadn't I? And she hadn't even known she wanted a dog.

"Mr. Brown has been waiting for Shep," Bev said. "He raised border collies years ago and is excited to be near one again. He is in a wheelchair. I thought it might be best if we left him in his room until he felt comfortable with Shep."

I had seen only one other person in a wheelchair—Laura's father. We moved into Mr. Brown's room, where he was sitting in his chair with wheels.

Mr. Brown saw me and clapped his hands.

"My, Shep," he said, "you look a lot like my old dog, Patsy. She was a wonderful herding dog. Come over here."

Mr. Brown patted his thigh. Laura unhooked my leash, and I hurried over to the old man. He reached behind my ears and along my back. His hands were gentle but probably didn't work as well as they had when he was younger. I licked his hand as he held it in front of me.

"Such a handsome dog. Does he work sheep or cattle?" Mr. Brown asked Laura.

Laura shook her head and replied that I could possibly become a champion Frisbee player. Mr. Brown smiled and patted my head. Laura explained to Mr. Brown that she needed to go down the hall for a few minutes and asked if it would be all right if I stayed in the room with him. Mr. Brown was delighted. I loved the extra attention.

Laura snapped on my leash and gave the loose end to Mr. Brown. She left the room with the door to the hallway open.

I sat beside Mr. Brown, content to be with him until Laura returned.

Mr. Brown and I were not alone for long. An elderly woman peeked into the room and saw the two of us. I wagged my tail in greeting. She smiled and asked Mr. Brown if she could come closer.

"Certainly. Come on in," Mr. Brown said. The woman shuffled into the room.

As she stood beside me, I sat up, wagged my tail, and lifted my head to her waiting hands. I saw tears in her eyes.

"You're such a pretty dog," she said, "much larger than my little Misty. I had Misty for almost ten years, but I had to give her up when I moved in here. My great-niece has her now. I wish I could see Misty again, but she lives in another state."

I noticed how difficult it was for her to move. It seemed that most of the people in the building moved slowly, if they moved at all. It dawned on me that in all the rooms in this huge building, there must be older people who couldn't take care of themselves. I wondered how Laura found out about the nursing home.

Mr. Brown motioned to a chair near his bed. The woman he called Mrs. Stiles pulled it toward us and sat down. I stayed between the two of them so both Mr. Brown and Mrs. Stiles could pet me.

It seemed important to them to touch me.

During the next fifteen minutes or so, several other elderly men and women entered the room, until it was almost filled wall-to-wall with people. Mr. Brown dropped my leash and let me greet each person who entered the room. Everyone seemed delighted to see me.

I worked my way around the crowd, returning every few minutes to assure Mr. Brown that I was behaving myself—and indeed I was. One woman offered me a chocolate crème cookie. Laura never let me eat chocolate, so I politely turned away, but I licked her frail, white hand.

"See, he's been taught not to accept food from strangers," Mr. Brown said.

"And that's a good thing," Mrs. Stiles added, "or he might leave here with a big stomachache."

Almost every hair on my body had been stroked by the time Laura and Bev returned to Mr. Brown's room. Laura barely had enough room to stand comfortably.

Laura smiled at everyone and hugged several of the residents as she made her way to my side. She explained that she and I were leaving to visit some of the residents who couldn't get out of their rooms. The people gathered in Mr. Brown's room thought that was a wonderful idea. Many of them gave me a final hug and invited me to come back soon. I thought we might.

Laura led me down the hallway. We turned into another hallway and stopped at a room with a high hospital bed.

A tiny older woman lay in the bed, her body propped up by pillows. She seemed to be asleep, but when Laura called her name—Mrs. Taylor—she opened her eyes and turned her head to find Laura and me.

Laura explained that she had brought me to visit her, as she had requested, and asked if I should come closer to the bed.

Mrs. Taylor nodded. Laura gently urged me forward. Mrs. Taylor dropped her arm to the side of the bed and motioned for me to come to her. She reached down and petted my head, saying over and over again, "Good dog, good dog."

Mrs. Taylor's voice wasn't loud. I knew from the sound of it that she was pleased to have me at her bedside. She whispered, "I haven't had a dog since I was a little girl. I always had cats."

I backed away a few steps. Cats were not my favorite creatures. Mrs. Taylor glanced up at Laura and then spoke to me.

"Oh my, Shep, I've said the wrong thing. What I meant, my dear, was that cats were the best pets for me. I always lived in apartments in a city. Even raised my family in one. I wanted my children to know and to love animals, and whenever we could, we had a cat or two around. My great-grandchildren have cats. A dog would be nice. Even a dog on my bed."

I turned my head back and forth as I listened to Mrs. Taylor. To jump on her bed would be a challenge for many dogs. Not for me, of course. I jump higher than that for a Frisbee. I stood quietly while Mrs. Taylor continued to pet me. After a few moments, her hand stopped moving and she brought it back to her bed. She smiled at me.

"I'm really tired now, Shep. Thank you so much for coming to see me. I need a little nap."

Laura snapped on my leash and quietly led me from Mrs. Taylor's room. I would have stayed longer. Mrs. Taylor seemed to need someone close to her.

Laura knelt beside me in the hallway. "You were such a good dog with Mrs. Taylor. She was the first one to ask for you. She's very ill, and her family is far away. I'm so glad we could visit with her today."

We started down the hall to another room. Suddenly, an elderly man, moving on stiff legs and trying to manage a cane, hurried down the hall toward us. He struggled to keep his balance as he approached Laura and me. His shouting echoed through the hall.

"That dog! Get that dog out of here! I pay too much money to this place to have a dog running loose up and down the halls. Probably doesn't even have a license."

My Border Collie World

The angry man hobbled right up to Laura. I stood my ground between him and Laura. I may have even curled my lip at him to show my teeth. Laura reacted immediately.

"It's OK, Shep. Everything's all right. Stay calm." I listened to her but moved closer to her side.

A woman in a white uniform scurried toward us as Laura and the man faced each other.

"Mr. Welch," the woman spoke sternly, "Shep has permission to be here. They wouldn't be in the hall if he didn't. Several of the patients asked Laura to bring him for the Christmas party. Shep won't hurt you."

Mr. Welch kept complaining.

"Dogs carry germs. We'll catch our death of something from his germs."

I was beginning to resent Mr. Welch. I was clean. I'd even endured the self-wash dog place the day before and played in the white snow early that morning. I tried to stare down Mr. Welch, like I often did to cats, but Laura gave me a tug on my leash.

I stepped behind Laura. What did this angry old man mean about not having a license? Somewhere under the bells and the bow, my license jingled. Laura never would have brought me without my license. I didn't like Mr. Welch.

We were joined by an important-looking man in a business suit who took Mr. Welch aside and spoke to him with authority.

"Mr. Welch, I assure you that Shep's presence does not pose a threat of injury or illness to our residents. Many asked if we might have animals visit during Christmas week. Laura brought Shep because we asked her to do so."

Laura and I looked at each other, wondering what would happen next. From down the hall, another elderly lady wheeled her chair right up to Mr. Welch. In fact, she moved up from behind and ran right into him.

"Ralph, how dare you interrupt our special time with visitors with your harsh words?"

Mr. Welch caught his balance and backed away from the woman. She again pushed her wheelchair toward him.

"I'm ashamed of you, Ralph. This was my idea, and since this is my nursing home, I suggest that you apologize to Laura and Shep right now."

Mr. Welch glanced at Laura and then at me. He took off down the hall faster than he had approached us, despite his stiff legs.

Laura thanked the lady, whom she addressed as Mrs. Howe.

"Pay no attention to Ralph. He's a miserable old man who can't stand to see anyone getting any enjoyment out of life. Come now. Let's go down to the dining room. We'll distribute the gifts your church sent."

Mrs. Howe reached out and gently took my leash. I moved as close to her as I could and licked her hand. She was my rescuer today. It didn't take me long to learn to stay out of the way of her wheelchair as we all moved down the hall to the dining room.

I counted twelve tables, with several residents sitting at each one. One entire side of the dining room was glass, and I could see the lawn outside covered with snow. Viewing all those shrubs and trees caused me to think about going outside, but Laura shook her head as she watched me.

"No," she said firmly. "We'll be leaving soon."

I retreated to the side of Mrs. Howe's wheelchair. She stroked my back.

"Laura, how do you wish to distribute the gifts?" Mrs. Howe asked.

Laura suggested that either she or a staff member reach into the pile and retrieve a gift. Each one had been marked for either a man or a woman, and the church had supplied enough for everyone.

"All the residents have been given a number," Laura said, "so we'll call a number. The person who has that number will raise a hand, and we'll take the gift to him or her."

Laura picked up the first gift. "If you're a woman and you have number one, this is your gift," Laura announced.

A woman in a wheelchair toward the back of the room held up her card with the number one on it.

"That's me," she said.

Laura started toward her, gift in hand.

The woman stopped Laura. "Oh, please, let the dog come with you. I want to pet him."

Mrs. Howe released my leash. I followed Laura to the woman who held up her hand. When we were at the wheelchair, Laura gave the small package to me, and I handed it to the woman. The room burst into cheers. The woman leaned over and petted me. I moved as close to her as the wheelchair would allow.

Most of the residents wanted me to be part of the delivery crew. Laura took off my leash.

"OK, Shep. You go with Bev or me to deliver the packages."

I wagged my tail to let Laura know I understood what was expected of me. The three of us delivered the rest of the gifts.

I visited every table in the room before all the gifts were distributed. One of the last gifts was for a man, number thirty. I was surprised when Mr. Welch raised his hand from the back of the room. Laura started to take the gift to him, but he shook his head and pointed to me. I carefully carried the package and stopped a few feet away from Mr. Welch.

Mr. Welch motioned for me to come closer, and I slowly moved toward him. When I stood right in front of him, he carefully took the package from me and said, "Thank you, Shep." I wagged my tail and trotted back to Laura as Mrs. Howe cheered.

After the gifts were distributed, the staff served a meal—roast beef, mashed potatoes and gravy, and some kind of vegetable. I wagged my tail as a platter was carried past me, but Laura shook her head. A man at the table nearest to me spoke.

"Shep can have my meat. I'd rather he have it."

The dining room manager heard the man's offer and hurried over to stop the man from feeding his meal to me.

"Mr. Simpson, I have a special plate for Shep. You eat your food. I know roast beef is one of your favorites."

"Are you sure Shep will get some roast beef?"

The manager assured Mr. Simpson that I would. I did and enjoyed every bite.

When we left the nursing home, I felt it had been a special day. The snow was lightly falling as we approached the truck. Laura gave me a big hug and a treat before opening the passenger-side door for me.

Over the years, Laura and I spent many hours with the residents in the nursing home. That first Christmas visit was my favorite.

CHAPTER 6

Being a Good Neighbor

I LIKED OUR next-door neighbors, Marv and Eleanor Merrill, from the first time I met them shortly after Laura brought me home from the shelter.

Laura told me about them before we got acquainted. Our front door and front lawn faced the Merrills' carport. Marv walked along our fence when he retrieved his morning paper.

Marv and Eleanor were delighted to have me as a neighbor. Maybe they thought I was a watchdog. The Merrills had lived in the mobile-home park for more than thirty years. They had owned two dogs during that time. At the time I met the Merrills, they were probably the oldest people I had ever known. Some of the people I met at the nursing home were probably older. Marv and Eleanor were fortunate to be able to move around well enough to stay in their own home.

Eleanor used a walker to steady herself when she moved around the house. She explained to me that using the walker was the reason they hadn't adopted another dog. They were afraid they might stumble over a pet. I was careful to stay out of the walker's way when I visited.

I was pleased that Marv spent much of the daytime in the backyard of his home. He would work on his car or in the shed, where he kept his tools. I liked my yard, and it was nice to have male company.

Marv watched me catch a Frisbee soon after we met. He clapped his hands and moved over to the fence to watch Laura and me play. I picked up my Frisbee and took it over to the fence in front of him and dropped it. Marv stretched to reach over the fence to retrieve the Frisbee, but he couldn't quite reach it.

I picked up the Frisbee and held it up for Marv. He grabbed the Frisbee and threw it for me. Marv was the only person who would get the Frisbee right to his hands. I would give it to him like a retriever, not a herder.

Laura often watched out the window or door when Marv and I played. She shook her head at how carefully I handed the Frisbee to Marv. Sometimes, Marv would give me treats when I made a spectacular catch.

Marv and Eleanor helped me be comfortable. If I stayed outside and it started to rain or snow, I rushed to the door to get back into the house. They made certain Laura would open the door for me. If I stood for more than a minute or two, one of them would call Laura on her phone and tell her I wanted to go into the house. Whatever she was doing, Laura stopped long enough to let me in. She was aware the Merrills meant business when it came to caring for me.

Marv and Eleanor's son and daughter-in-law visited often. The old man across the street never had visitors. The only person I saw at his home was the paper boy, who also mowed his lawn in the summer and shoveled his sidewalk when it snowed in the winter. He drove a huge older car. I wondered how he could tell where he was going. His head didn't seem high enough for him to see over the car's dashboard. I thought he must be lonely and wondered why he didn't get a dog for company.

During my second winter with Laura, Marv rescued an abandoned half-grown kitten. He fixed it a nice bed in his shed. I watched Marv feed it and often stood at the fence while he took care of the kitten. As much as I didn't like cats, I was glad Marv fixed a home for the stray kitten.

January turned so cold that ice didn't melt on the sidewalks and streets during the day. I saw people slip on the ice that seemed to be everywhere.

On quiet winter nights, Laura and I rarely heard noise. If I did hear something unusual, I would wake Laura, and she would let me go outside to investigate.

Whether it was only the noise or also my instinct, I sensed something strange was happening outside about five o'clock one January morning. I woke Laura. She grabbed her robe and let me out the front door. It was still dark. Only one streetlight shone in the area. I traveled a few feet across the front yard when I heard, "Help, help," a muffled, desperate cry from near the corner of our yard.

My ears sprang forward. I listened intently as I hurried in the direction of the cry. I found the source.

Marv lay on the ground near his newspaper box. He always went out early to pick up his morning paper. I rushed to the fence, as close to him as I could get.

Marv was lying on his side, weak, scared, cold, and unable to move.

"Shep, get Laura. I need help. I'm hurt and freezing. Go get Laura."

I began barking, big time. For a few moments, I stood close to Marv as I barked. I then ran to the house, barking all the way. Laura opened the door and yelled.

"Shep, stop that barking. You'll wake the whole neighborhood."

I continued barking, and Laura stepped outside on the landing. I quit barking for a moment.

"Laura, help me. I've fallen." Marv's faint, frightened voice carried to Laura. She hurried behind me to the fence in her robe and slippers and saw Marv.

Laura leaned beside Marv and gently touched him.

"Hang in there, Marv. I'm calling nine one one. I'll get some blankets out here."

"I think my hip is broken," Marv whispered.

"Don't move. I'll be right back. We'll take care of you."

Laura rushed into the house, called the emergency number, grabbed her bedding, and ran back to Marv.

I ran out the gate with Laura and stood near Marv while she covered him with the bedding.

"Stay with us, Marv. The ambulance is on its way."

"What about Eleanor?" he whispered.

"I'll wake her and drive her to the hospital."

Moments later, the flashing lights of the ambulance appeared. Laura guided the crew to Marv. I stood quietly out of the way while the EMTs did their work. Time crept by. Marv cried out in pain a couple of times, but the EMTs were doing all they could for him.

As soon as the ambulance left, Laura entered Eleanor's bedroom and gently woke her. She explained to Eleanor what had happened. Laura told her she would drive her to the hospital. Eleanor climbed out of bed to get dressed. Laura called Eleanor's son, Luke, as she went home to get herself dressed. He said he would meet them at the hospital.

When Laura helped Eleanor into the truck, Eleanor insisted that I come along. Laura hesitated, but Eleanor scooted over so there would be room for me on the seat. I jumped in beside her.

Luke and his wife were waiting at the hospital. Laura and I were not needed anymore. Luke hugged Eleanor, Laura, and me. He thanked me again and again. I felt like a hero.

Marv had broken his hip after slipping on a patch of ice. It took him months to completely recover from the injury.

Weeks later, Laura answered our doorbell and found Marv on the steps with his walker. His family surrounded him. Laura and I greeted each one and invited them all into the living room.

Luke presented Laura with a gold-bordered certificate. I thought it was more impressive than her university degree. Laura took the certificate, leaned down, and read the words to me.

The heading read, "Our Hero Dog Shep." Beneath the heading was the story of my early-morning effort. I wagged my tail while everyone made a fuss over me. The grandkids had brought me treats. I strutted a bit around the room. But, really, why all the fuss? I was just being a good neighbor.

Chapter 7

Family Challenges

Maybe because of Marv's traumatic fall on the ice or perhaps because winter dragged into mid-March, I eagerly waited for spring. As soon as she dared, Laura planted petunias, pansies, and other flowering plants around our yard.

Spring also meant that Laura was away from the house more but seldom overnight. One spring afternoon, she called me to the house.

"Shep, I'm running over to Danville to follow up on a story. I'm leaving you in the house."

Laura had been gone for about an hour when I heard the back door open. Strange. I left my bed and headed for the kitchen. It couldn't be Laura returning. Who, then?

Laura's nephew, Brad, stood at the entrance to the kitchen.

We discovered each other at the same time.

"Shep," he spoke quietly. "I didn't know you were here."

I approached Brad cautiously. He sounded nervous, like we both knew he shouldn't be there.

Brad reached down and petted me as he walked through the house. As he headed toward Laura's bedroom, I stayed right at his heels even though he tried to brush me back. He entered Laura's bedroom, and I barked. He had never gone in there when Laura was home. Why should he be there when she was gone?

Brad stared at me for a moment. I stood my ground. He slowly backed out of Laura's bedroom. He stepped toward Laura's office. I followed him.

Brad opened a drawer in Laura's desk. I barked again, louder this time. He slammed the drawer shut and glanced at Laura's laptop. He reached toward it, and I growled.

What he did next frightened me. He picked up a paperweight from the desk and raised his arm while staring right into my eyes. I crouched. Did he plan to throw it at me?

I heard rather than saw Brad put the paperweight back onto the desk. He brushed past me on his way out of the office and kept moving until he stumbled out the back door and closed it behind him. I stood at the door wondering what I would do if Brad returned before Laura came home.

Brad's visit was weird. No one had driven him to our home. He had ridden his bicycle. I watched the teenager ride out of our mobile-home park and wished that Laura would get back soon. What odd behavior from Brad. I had never seen him nervous or scary before.

Laura returned late in the afternoon. I was relieved to have her home. Her arrival always made my world all right again.

Soon afterward, Laura's cell phone rang. It was her sister, Marj.

"No, Marj. I haven't seen or heard from Brad. Why?"

Laura frowned as she listened to her sister. Marj explained that Brad hadn't come home from school. She wasn't sure he had even gone to school.

I wished I could talk and tell Laura that Brad had been there and probably not for a good reason.

After Laura finished her conversation with Marj, she spoke to me.

"Shep, Brad didn't come home from school today and hasn't been in touch with his mother. I'm worried. Marj is still having a rough time adjusting to being a single mom. Maybe she's being a bit too strict with the kids."

Before she went to bed, Laura received a message from Marj that Brad had come home. He had had trouble with his bicycle.

The next day, Laura brought home a surprise from her trip to town. Her ten-year-old niece, Connie, climbed out of the truck. She carried a small suitcase.

Laura explained Connie's presence to me.

"Shep, Connie has tomorrow off from school, so she'll spend the day and the weekend with us."

I wagged my tail as I greeted Connie. She was a good Frisbee thrower, for a girl, and she didn't seem to tire of playing with me.

We had another visitor that day. Before dinner, Connie's father, Sam, drove into our driveway. Laura greeted him at the door.

Sam worked as an investigator for the district attorney's office. He had left Marj and the kids before Laura and I found each other. Marj was bitter about the subsequent divorce and the other woman involved. I was certainly aware that Marj was unhappy and that she didn't like animals. I wondered if she liked anyone but her kids anymore.

Connie rushed to her father, and they embraced. With Sam's work schedule and the restrictive court visitation limits, father and daughter didn't get to spend much time together.

I chose to lie down a little distance from the group. Laura wore a sad smile as she watched father and daughter.

Laura offered Sam a cup of coffee or tea or a glass of wine. He politely declined all three.

"Laura, I need to talk with you."

Connie sensed this would be adult talk. She agreed to go to Laura's bedroom if she could have cookies and milk. Laura fixed a tray, and Connie took it into her room.

I lay close to Sam and Laura. I wanted to find out what was going on in my family.

Laura poured herself a cup of coffee and motioned for Sam to join her at the kitchen table.

Sam told Laura that he had been offered a promotion with the federal government. He wanted the job. Accepting it would mean he would be leaving the state. He surprised Laura by saying he would be going alone. He had broken up with the other woman.

Laura asked if there was any chance he would go back to his family. Sam shook his head. He and Marj had serious problems before the affair, and neither wanted a reconciliation.

Sam carefully told Laura that he was deeply worried about his son. Brad had started skipping school and may have taken a few items from his home. While Sam didn't believe the teenager was into drugs or alcohol, his behavior raised red flags.

If I could have talked, I would have let them know that I agreed Sam should have concerns. Brad's visit to our home could have ended quite differently if I hadn't been there.

"So, Sam, what are you going to do?"

"You know your sister better than anyone else. Do you think she would let me take Brad with me?"

Laura slowly put her cup down and looked directly at Sam.

"You mean permanently?"

"I honestly don't know. School will be out soon. I'm thinking we could try it for the summer. The city offers a lot of activities for boys in the summer."

"What about your new job? You've always worked long hours and lots of overtime. Would Brad feel abandoned?"

"That's another positive about the job. It's mostly training. I'd work a normal schedule. Weekends and holidays off—vacation I could really take."

"How much have you told Marj?"

"Not a lot. Marj knows I'm thinking about the job. She was angry at first that I might be leaving the area and the kids behind. I sense she would be more cooperative now. The past month with Brad has been difficult for her."

"What's next?"

"I'm meeting Marj and Brad this weekend while Connie is with you. Afterward, we'll bring Connie into the mix."

"Is this why Marj suggested Connie spend the weekend with me?"

"Yes. I'm picking up Brad. He and I will spend a couple of days together. Depending on how that goes, we'll all make some decisions, hopefully ones that are the best possible for everyone."

Laura glanced at me and then at Sam. "I'll pray for all of you."

Sam stood and moved from the table. I hurried to Laura's bedroom. Connie was standing at the door and dropped to her knees to hug me. I licked her face and tasted the salt of her tears. I didn't know how much of the conversation she had heard.

She was still hugging me when Sam entered the room. Connie left me and hugged her father.

Connie and I spent the weekend together. I slept beside her bed each night. She would reach down often and stroke my head. I thought she even did it in her sleep.

Laura worked all weekend at her computer. Something about a Monday-morning deadline. Connie and I played outside. Laura brought Connie my leash a couple of times, and we retrieved the mail.

Laura didn't trust me to go to the mailbox without my leash because one time I chased a cat across the street and was almost hit by a car.

The weekend ended with a surprise. Marj called Laura and invited all three of us to a picnic in a city park before she brought Connie home. Connie danced around the living room when she heard the news. Then she hugged me. I was the "whatever-happens-hug-Shep" dog for Connie, whether she was happy, sad, or excited. I loved it!

Marj met us at the park. She hugged Laura and Connie and even patted me on the head. I was pleased that she was glad to see us all. She cheerfully spread out the lunch.

After we ate, Connie and I went to play. Marj and Laura stayed behind to clean up and to talk. Laura briefed me on the conversation later.

Laura told me that Marj, Brad, and Sam had met for dinner the night before. Brad agreed that continuing his behavior could jeopardize the rest of his teenage years and beyond. He acknowledged that the divorce had affected him deeply. He had to accept losing a huge part of his dad as well as having to live with his bitter, depressed mother. Both parents acknowledged they had not been sensitive enough to the traumatic effect the divorce had on their children.

When Sam explained his job offer and his desire to take Brad with him, Marj and Brad were stunned. The three finally concluded that Brad would finish the school year, and if his grades and behavior were satisfactory, he could choose where to spend the summer and perhaps a longer time.

As Connie and I returned to the picnic table, I noticed that Marj and Laura had been crying, but both seemed OK. Marj patted the seat next to her. Connie sat down. Marj wrapped her arms around her daughter and told her about the weekend.

After Marj finished, Connie quietly knelt in the grass and hugged me. I licked her face.

The next afternoon, Laura and I relaxed on our patio in the spring warmth. We were startled as Brad approached on his bike. Neither of us expected Brad.

I stood between Laura and Brad, not sure of Brad's intentions.

My aggressive position puzzled Laura.

"Shep, it's Brad. You know him. Relax."

"Aunt Laura, if I were Shep, I wouldn't relax. I stopped by to tell you I went into your house the other day when I knew you weren't home."

"Brad, you're always welcome at my home."

"Not that day, Aunt Laura. I thought about taking something of yours—even stealing your laptop. Shep wouldn't let me touch anything."

"But why?"

"I was upset, angry—at Mom, at a teacher. I thought about stealing some things I could sell and running away."

"You've had a rough time, Brad."

"Aunt Laura. I shouldn't have done that. Shep stopped me from doing something foolish. I'm sorry, and I want to tell Shep I'm sorry."

Laura stepped over and hugged Brad. "I know you are. Life is going to get better—for your whole family. Shep understands, don't you, Shep?"

I wasn't so sure. I cocked my head at Brad but stood my ground.

"Come on, Shep. He's sorry."

I wagged my tail and stepped toward Brad. He knelt down and hugged me. I licked his face.

I missed Brad when he left that summer, mostly because we spent quite a bit of time together before school was out.

I chased my Frisbee hundreds of times as he threw it to me in a neighboring football field. When Brad left with his father, Marj, Laura, Connie, and I became closer.

Brad did not return in the fall. We all missed him. Laura often read his e-mails to me. He had discovered soccer and was playing on the school team.

One Saturday in early fall, Marj invited Laura and me over for lunch. An excited Connie ran out to our truck as we pulled into her driveway. She carried a squirming puppy, laughing and squeezing it as she approached us.

Thank goodness it was a border collie.

CHAPTER 8

Our Guest

LIFE WAS ALMOST perfect for me. I convinced myself that I was in charge of the house, the truck, and Laura. Every morning and every evening, Laura placed food and water in a kitchen corner. She always made certain I also had a bowl of fresh water outside.

I had more Frisbees than I could catch, and I even chose which one I wanted to chase. I ran freely around my fenced yard and enjoyed frequent trips to Grey Wings.

On the not-so-perfect column, baths were a nuisance, although I loved water in about any other situation, and the annual trip to the veterinarian was not pleasant. I also didn't like spending much time at the boarding kennel. Laura didn't take me there often, but she explained that she couldn't always drive her truck on assignment and would fly on an airplane instead. The airport was only a few miles from our home. She always brought me back a special treat. After a week of moping around the house, I forgave Laura for leaving me.

Laura had found the best boarding kennel in the area. The Barkley Boarding Kennels were located outside the city limits. The family who owned the kennels raised border collies and Jack Russell terriers as well as horses, so I had plenty of company. A teenage son and daughter gave me extra attention. I shouldn't complain. I simply wasn't the most important creature in the world when I stayed at the kennel. I felt I was when I was with Laura.

One summer day, I faced a huge, although temporary, change in my life. Laura left me home and took my leash with her. She had never done that before. I ran to the door to meet her when she came home.

I smelled another dog. I barked. I heard her speak softly to the dog. That upset me, and I barked louder. Laura opened the door, and trailing behind her was an older golden retriever.

The retriever hunched down like it was afraid. I cautiously moved forward to get a better smell. The dog was a female. Laura greeted me as usual and explained why she had brought another dog into our home.

"Shep, her name is Goldie. Her person is in the hospital. We're going to take care of Goldie for a while."

What did "for a while" mean? And what did "take care of her" mean? This was my home. I didn't take care of dogs, and Laura took care of only me. Goldie wagged her tail at me. I didn't pay much attention. Laura announced that she would bring Goldie's bed into the house and we would all get acquainted.

As Laura started out the door, Goldie trailed at her heels. They weren't going anywhere without me, so all three of us moved out to the truck.

Laura brought in a large dog bed. I had a dog bed, too, but I seldom used it. I slept anywhere and everywhere I pleased, usually in an ancient recliner that I thought Laura bought at a thrift store especially for me. When I didn't use the recliner, I sometimes slept near the front door in case our home needed protection.

Laura made one more trip to the truck, alone, and brought the rest of Goldie's belongings into our house. She placed Goldie's food bowl and her water bowl across the room from mine. Did Laura think that would keep me from snooping to see what was in Goldie's bowls?

Laura poured water for Goldie, and the retriever eagerly drank most of it. She placed food in Goldie's other bowl, but Goldie was not interested in food. I, on the other hand, was delighted to see the full bowl. I had eaten all of my food hours earlier.

I sniffed around Goldie's food bowl. Laura warned me to get away from it. It was not my food. So? I moved to Goldie's bowl once more, and Laura scolded me. I dropped my ears, tucked my tail between my legs, and backed away. Laura seldom raised her voice at me. She had just done it twice within a few minutes.

The afternoon dragged by. I was not a happy dog. When Laura went outside to work in her flower bed, Goldie followed right behind her. I ran and grabbed my Frisbee and dropped it at Laura's feet. She stopped digging and threw my Frisbee.

I jumped high into the air to catch it. Actually, I was showing off. Goldie was not impressed. She quietly glanced at the Frisbee and then at me. She reminded me of my neighbor beagle, Bart, who never paid attention to my Frisbee antics.

When bedtime arrived, I was not happy that Goldie was still with us. Laura must have sensed my mood. I climbed into my recliner and ignored them both. Laura sat at my feet, with Goldie a few yards away.

"Shep," Laura said, "we may have Goldie as our guest for about a month. Her person needs time to recover from surgery. She has no one else to care for Goldie."

Laura said Goldie was ten years old and that her person, Ann, had found Goldie when she was a puppy.

It would have broken Ann's heart to give up Goldie because of the surgery. Ann hoped she would be able to keep Goldie after she recovered, but even that wasn't certain.

Laura reached up and hugged me and asked me to be a good host.

Laura took Goldie's bed into her bedroom and placed it near her own bed. I objected to that. I usually didn't sleep in Laura's room, but the thought of having another dog in her bedroom disturbed me. I was jealous.

Goldie still hadn't eaten by the time we all went to bed. After Goldie curled up in her bed, I sneaked back into the kitchen and ate Goldie's meal. No sense in letting good food go to waste.

As I wandered through the house, I noticed that Laura had left her slippers in their usual place by the end of her bed.

I stood in the doorway of the bedroom for a few moments and then crept into the room. I picked up one slipper with my teeth and chewed on it for a while, and then I quietly dropped it near Goldie's bed. She must have been exhausted. She slept the whole time I was in the room. Laura never changed positions in her bed.

I wasn't sure why I did something so mean. I hadn't done a dirty trick like that before. I had to admit to myself that I wanted Goldie to get into trouble and even hoped she would be put outside at night.

The next morning, Laura climbed out of bed and reached for her slippers. When she realized one had been badly chewed, she yelled, "Goldie!"

The retriever arose from her bed and hurried to Laura's side.

"Goldie," Laura scolded, waving the damaged slipper in Goldie's face. "Look what you did to my slipper. Bad girl."

Confused and hurt, Goldie stared at Laura. I quietly made my way into the bedroom and stood in the doorway, innocently wagging my tail. Goldie looked like someone had struck her as Laura continued to wave the slipper in her face. Then she tucked her tail between her legs and slowly walked back to her bed, turning her back on Laura.

Laura put on her robe and moved into the kitchen. The coffee was brewing. Laura headed for the back door with me at her feet. She paused when she noticed Goldie's food bowl was empty and shot an inquiring look at me. Goldie slunk slowly out of the bedroom when Laura called to her.

"Time to go outside, Goldie." Laura's voice wavered when she spoke to the retriever. Goldie wagged her tail slowly and followed me out to the yard.

Laura picked up our two water bowls, emptied them, and refilled each with fresh water. She glanced out the window and watched Goldie and me in the yard.

I led Goldie over to meet Bart, the beagle next door. He wagged his tail and greeted her through the fence. Bart acted as if Goldie was a dog he would like to know better—maybe a new friend.

I trotted back toward the house. Goldie chose to stay outside and lie down next to the fence close to Bart. She must have been looking for a friend. I felt guilty.

Goldie, Laura, and I went to Grey Wings that day. I chased my Frisbee, splashed in the ponds, and thoroughly enjoyed the time we spent there. Goldie stayed close to Laura, who often stroked Goldie and kept telling her she was a good dog. Maybe Laura felt she had reacted too harshly about the slipper.

That night, Goldie's bed was placed outside Laura's room and down the hall. I was pleased. To me it meant that Goldie didn't have the same place in Laura's heart that she had before the slipper incident. I curled up in my recliner and went to sleep.

The next morning, I awoke to find Laura standing above me, hands on her hips, frowning. Beside my recliner lay a shredded embroidered kitchen towel. Laura picked it up and shook it in my face.

"Shep, how could you? This is one of my favorite kitchen towels. Just because Goldie chewed up a slipper, you didn't need to tear up something of mine, too. Shame on you!"

Goldie was still sleeping down the hall. She didn't move.

Laura opened the back door and motioned for me to go outside. I was embarrassed. I was guilty. Oh, not of chewing up the towel. I never would have done that, but for what I had done to Goldie.

Goldie trotted outside later and immediately headed to the back of the fence to visit with Bart. I caught up with her in the middle of the yard.

I stood right in front of her and confessed about the slipper. The only excuse I had to offer was that maybe I was jealous of the attention Laura paid to her.

Goldie placed her head across my neck and whispered that she felt especially fortunate that Laura had agreed to care for her. Not many people would have taken such an old dog, even temporarily. She said I was lucky to have Laura all the time, this big yard, and Grey Wings.

I couldn't respond, so I joined her on her visit to Bart.

I turned my head to see Laura standing at the top of the steps. She waved to us, letting us know that she watched Goldie and me talk. I think she knew what had happened with the slipper and the towel.

That night, Goldie left her bed and slept beside me near the front door. Laura found us the next morning. She smiled and added a treat for each of us at breakfast. I decided she really did figure out what had happened between Goldie and me and knew we were both sorry.

Goldie stayed with us longer than a month. Her person, Ann Reynolds, joined us until she was strong enough to care for herself. Ann was kind to me and was grateful to have a place where she and Goldie could stay together.

When Ann became well enough to go with us, we all spent time at Grey Wings. Goldie barked encouragement when I chased Frisbees. Maybe she wished she could join me.

Goldie took on an important job. She encouraged Ann to stretch and work her muscles. Goldie would drop items just out of Ann's reach so she had to work to get them. The two were a fine team.

The day Ann and Goldie left us, Ann's son came. The family decided that Ann shouldn't live alone any longer nor live so far away from her family. She and Goldie would move to her son's home. Goldie accepted the move when Ann told her that the son's home had a large fenced yard.

I never saw Goldie after she and Ann moved. But whenever Laura received an e-mail from Ann, she would share it with me.

Goldie taught me a couple of valuable lessons. First, if you're going to pull a dirty trick on someone, be sure he or she isn't as smart or smarter than you are, and, second, more than one dog can live happily in a home. I was glad Goldie and Ann lived with us for a while.

Chapter 9

Sideswiped

Laura and I traveled in her truck for business and for pleasure. As a freelance writer, she sometimes would deliver her finished products to her clients. She took me along whenever she could.

During the hottest summer months, July and August, I usually would stay home. Even though the truck had air conditioning, the sun glared through the windows, and I could get too hot while she met with her clients. I was safe and comfortable at home and always had an adequate supply of food and water.

When I rode with Laura, she always fastened her seat belt and my harness in the front seat of the truck. The straps fit around my body and snapped me to into the seat belt at my side. I could curl up and lie down next to Laura if I positioned myself correctly. I wasn't nearly as interested in where she was going as she was. In fact, I was content to sleep most of the journey and be awakened when we arrived at our destination.

Occasionally, we visited her friends in another state and stayed overnight. We would sleep either in the bed of the truck or in a pet-friendly motel. Laura bought a truck tent, which gave us enough room to be comfortable. I was pleased that many motels welcomed or at least tolerated pets, although I couldn't imagine anyone wanting to travel anywhere with a cat.

When we traveled, I could easily land in my seat with one smooth leap from the ground. Laura would open the door on my side and finish what she was doing, knowing I would jump into the truck whenever we were ready to leave.

One September afternoon, we were returning from a visit with Laura's friends at their cabin in the mountains. We were on a two-lane mountain highway. I didn't like cars traveling toward us, even though I was aware they had their own side of the road. I didn't sleep when we were driving through the mountains and sat upright. Laura kept her headlights on so that approaching vehicles could see us better.

I stared out the windshield as two cars approached us traveling faster than they should. Suddenly, the second car tried to pass the first one and swerved right into our lane. Surely he would see us and move back into the other lane, but he didn't. Laura desperately tried to move off the highway to stay out of the car's way, but there wasn't room. A guardrail prevented Laura from driving off the road.

I saw and felt the crash as the car smashed into Laura's side of the truck. It wasn't quite a head-on crash, but it was bad enough. I was vaguely aware of the deafening sound of crashing metal. My head slammed against the door, and everything went black.

When I regained consciousness, I was lying on my side on a high table. I tried to lift my head. Pain shot through me, so I laid my head back down. After a few minutes, I struggled to get up, but two people held me firmly on the table.

"Shep, lie still. Just lie still. You're going to be OK."

I recognized the voice of Dr. Raines, my veterinarian. She stood beside me in her white jacket and stroked the top of my head.

"You've been in a bad accident, Shep," she said, "but you're going to be all right. You need to rest awhile longer."

I glanced around and realized I was in Dr. Raines's exam room. How did I get there? What happened? Why did I hurt all over? I looked around the room as far as I could see from my position. I didn't see Laura. Where was she? Laura had always been with me when I came to see Dr. Raines.

Then I remembered, although my mind was still foggy. Our truck had been hit by another car or truck. I wasn't sure which. Someone must have lifted me out of the wreckage. No way could I have gotten out by myself with my harness securely buckled.

Dr. Raines spoke to me again.

"Thank goodness you had on your harness, Shep. It saved your life. Also lucky you were wearing your tags, with my name and phone number on them."

Dr. Raines gently stroked my head. "You and Laura were in a bad wreck. Some idiot sideswiped your truck. An off-duty paramedic stopped and pulled you out of the truck, read your tag, and brought you here."

I struggled again. Dr. Raines allowed me to get to my feet. I stood up and looked for Laura. I barked for her. Laura wasn't in the room.

"Shep, I know, I know, but Laura isn't here. She's in the hospital. She was badly injured in the wreck. You must stay here for a while. Now, please, lie down again."

With Dr. Raines's encouragement and gentle hands, I lay back down on the table. My Laura? In a hospital? How could I get to her?

I must have been given something to make me sleep because I dozed off right away.

When I woke up, Dr. Raines gently lifted me off the table. I stood on the floor and winced because I felt a sharp pain in my shoulder. I stumbled over to the door and scratched. I'd never scratched a door before. I wanted to get out of the clinic.

Dr. Raines's assistant brought a leash, snapped it on me, and gently urged me away from the door. No one understood. I wanted to go find Laura.

"Shep, we know you're worried about Laura, but you can't go to her. She's probably still in surgery. Come. We'll go to our temporary boarding place. You'll find something to eat and drink there."

Dr. Raines led me to one of the several dog runs in the back of the clinic. I was coaxed inside one and lay down. I wasn't steady on my legs yet.

"Shep, I'm going to call the Barkleys. I'll tell them about the wreck and that you are with me. I know they'll come right in and get you. You'll be more comfortable at their kennel."

I dropped off to sleep in spite of my worry about Laura and the other animal noise. I woke up to a familiar voice.

"Hi, Shep." Darla Barkley dashed across the room toward me. "Are you OK, fella?"

I wagged my tail and barked a couple of times to let Darla know I was all right.

"Shep, we're taking you to our home until Laura can come and get you or we can take you to her."

Darla opened the door, snapped on my leash, and led me outside to her station wagon.

I hesitated. I didn't want to get into another vehicle. I pulled back on the leash. Darla sneaked up behind me, swooped me into her arms, and dumped me into the back of the station wagon. I struggled, but Darla's kids held me firmly in the back seat.

I settled down a few blocks from the clinic, but I was not comfortable until the station wagon stopped at the Barkleys.

The Barkley family took me into their home, but I wanted to go outside. I stood at the door. Darla led me to the boarding area. I knew I would be more comfortable in the run where I usually stayed. I knew I would be staying there, but I didn't know how long.

Darla returned to the house and brought me a bed.

Darla's daughter, Carrie, later brought me food. She wasn't surprised that I wasn't hungry nor that I never even sampled my meal. She was pleased that I drank some water.

I lay on my bed, and Carrie dropped down beside me.

"Shep, Mom called the hospital a few minutes ago. Laura's recovering. She had a broken leg and internal injuries, and she's awake now. We're all praying for a quick recovery."

I reached my paw over and laid it on Carrie's arm.

"Laura called for a nurse as soon as she woke up. She asked about you. Mom asked the nurse to tell Laura as soon as she could that you are OK and are here with us."

I wagged my tail to let Carrie know I understood and that I was thankful for the good news. She reached over and gave me a big hug. My shoulder didn't hurt much after that, and the food Carrie handed to me tasted good. I was fortunate that my only injuries were deep bruising and a cut on my shoulder.

The Barkley kids, Carrie and David, managed to spend a lot of time with me while I was at their place. We ran around the ranch. I tried to play with their dogs, but my heart wasn't in it. I didn't eat much for several days. Darla didn't act concerned as long as I drank my water. Then one morning, I woke up hungry and ate everything in my bowl.

Darla entered the kennel and was pleased that I had cleaned up my food.

"Good dog, Shep. Especially since I'm taking you back to Dr. Raines for a checkup. She asked to see you again."

I hesitated before hopping into the station wagon. We drove past the hospital on our way to the clinic.

"Maybe I'll have a surprise for you on the way back, Shep."

Darla smiled at me. "I can't promise anything."

Dr. Raines examined me thoroughly, much more thoroughly than I liked as a male dog. A bit embarrassing from a female.

"Shep, you're doing great. Your bruising and laceration are healing nicely."

Darla chatted on her phone while Dr. Raines examined me. I didn't hear most of what she said, but I thought it was someone at the hospital.

Dr. Raines asked about Laura when Darla's conversation ended.

"Laura's doing even better than the doctors expected," Darla said. "Apparently, her rib cage and leg took most of the impact of the crash, and there wasn't much internal damage."

"Did they arrest the person who hit the truck?" Dr. Raines asked.

"Yes. Another driver saw what happened and followed him. The car was so damaged it quit a short distance away. Several people had noticed the car weaving recklessly for miles. Apparently, his alcohol level was twice what the state allows. I understand he's been in jail."

I wagged my tail and barked once at the news.

After we left the clinic, we drove toward the hospital but not past it. Darla turned into the visitors' lot and parked the station wagon.

"Shep, you'll have to stay here. I'm going to see Laura."

At the sound of "Laura," my ears sprang forward. I wanted to go with Darla.

Darla scolded me gently. "Shep, you know you can't go into the hospital with me."

I scrunched down into the seat, but then I stood up so I could watch Darla enter the hospital. Even if I couldn't go, it was good that Laura would have a visitor I knew. After what seemed a long time to me, Darla came out of the hospital.

She hurried to my side of the station wagon, opened the door, and grabbed my leash.

"Come on, Shep," she said with a grin. "I've a surprise for you."

Darla led me to the hospital's emergency entrance. I stood beside her. The large glass doors slid open, and a nurse pushing a wheelchair approached me.

The wheelchair's occupant shouted, "Shep!" I tried to drag Darla in her direction.

Laura! Never had I been so happy to see anyone.

Darla held my leash tightly. When I reached Laura, she leaned out of the wheelchair and gave me a big hug. I licked her face again and again.

A huge cast encircled her left leg. She looked tired, but we were together. Too soon, the nurse insisted that Laura go back to her room. She turned the wheelchair and pushed Laura toward the door.

Darla thanked the nurse. I barked once. I couldn't help it.

Following my visit to the hospital and knowing that Laura was recovering, I found that time passed more quickly at the Barkleys. The family showered me with more attention than they gave the other dogs, even their own. They knew how much I missed Laura.

Weeks passed, and one day I heard a strange car drive into the Barkleys. I didn't pay much attention to the visitors until I recognized one of the voices. Laura! I paced around in my run and barked as loudly as I could. Laura was here!

Laura leaned on her crutches as she hurried toward me. She stroked me through the bars of my run until the door was opened.

Darla found a leash, hooked it onto me, and led me out of the kennel. I rushed the few feet to Laura. She cautioned me to relax, and I tried.

Darla took my leash and led me to the car that brought Laura to me. I ignored Laura's friend who was driving. I wanted only Laura's attention.

Home had never looked as wonderful as when Laura and I returned to it. I couldn't remember a happier time in my entire life. Well, maybe when I'd found Laura.

The next morning, I noted our truck was not in the carport.

A part of my world was missing. I wandered around the yard. Laura watched as I sniffed every corner.

"Shep, we no longer have a truck. It was damaged beyond repair. It couldn't be fixed."

I wondered how we would manage without our truck.

Laura's leg continued to heal, and soon she grabbed only a cane once in a while.

One day, a strange man arrived at our door. Even stranger, Laura greeted him warmly and left with him. When Laura returned, she called to me.

"Come, Shep. We'll take Dan back to the car dealer. We've found ourselves new transportation. You'll like it."

As we drove into the dealership, someone was driving a Subaru Outback through the car wash.

"There is it, Shep. Our new vehicle."

Laura, the salesman, and I went inside the building. When we came out, she led me toward the Subaru. She told me it was not a new car, but it looked like it had been treated well.

I was happy to know we had another vehicle.

Laura led me to the passenger side, and I jumped in. I glanced over the seat and thought that sometimes I probably would choose the back seat but not today. I wanted to be Laura's copilot. She carefully buckled me into my new harness before she moved around to her side of the car.

As we drove out of the dealership, I leaned over and licked Laura's face. How fortunate we were to have survived that accident. I hoped the driver never got his license back or, even better, was in jail.

CHAPTER 10

Frisbee Competition

From the first time I caught a Frisbee, I knew that this colorful disk would be a favorite toy of mine. I attempted to catch my Frisbee from anyone who threw it. I learned that a person developed skill in throwing Frisbees. Catching a Frisbee came naturally—at least for me.

Children, young people, and even grandmas and grandpas enjoyed throwing Frisbees to me. I would never embarrass anyone by ignoring a badly thrown Frisbee. I would try to catch or at least pick up the Frisbee, even if it was badly thrown.

One of Laura's friends really liked me, but she never learned to throw a Frisbee the right way. I often found myself chasing the Frisbee along the ground, waiting for it to slow down or stop so I could retrieve it. Laura's friend always gave me lots of praise when I brought the Frisbee back to her.

When we were in a dog park or other public area, I liked watching other dogs chasing Frisbees. Laura often kept me on a leash because of the time we had been in a park and I had chased a Frisbee that I should have left alone.

The situation happened when we were strolling in the park and a white Frisbee flew my way, followed at a distance by a small, yappy white dog.

The Frisbee had traveled a long distance and would obviously land out of the range of the small dog. I ran after the disk, passed the little white dog, and caught the Frisbee before it hit the ground. It was one of my best leaping catches.

Laura ran toward me and in a loud voice demanded that I drop the Frisbee. The small, white dog stood a few feet away and was growling and barking. His person ran across the field toward us, shouting and waving his arms.

I dropped the Frisbee and wondered what I had done that was making everyone so angry.

Laura snapped the leash onto my collar and grabbed the Frisbee from in front of me. The small dog cautiously approached Laura. She handed him the Frisbee.

The dog's owner joined us. He had stopped yelling. Laura said she was sorry for my behavior and blamed it on my love of Frisbees. When she finished, the man smiled at her and patted my head.

The white dog gripped his Frisbee.

Laura and the man shook hands. I stood my ground when he leaned over and spoke to me.

"Hey, fella, you should enter the Frisbee competition here this Saturday. That was some catch."

Laura asked for more information about the competition. The man explained that the Frisbee competition was sponsored by a local pet store. Any dog whose owner had registered could compete. The competition was a fund raiser for the local animal shelter. Dogs that entered the competition received bandannas, and the owners got T-shirts promoting the event. I didn't like bandannas, but catching Frisbees and supporting the shelter appealed to me.

On Saturday morning, Laura and I traveled to the park, eager to join the competition. I wore my bandanna, and Laura's new T-shirt had an entry number pinned to the back.

We were number seventy-six. I saw several three-digit numbers. This was a big deal.

Laura brought three friends to cheer me on as I competed.

The section of the park prepared for the competition looked more like a football field with bleachers on either side and chalk lines marking distances so the judges could tell how far the dogs traveled to catch the Frisbee.

Laura's friends found seats in the bleachers. Laura and I stood in the competitors' lineup to wait our turn. I peeked around Laura's legs and eyed the competition. Each dog was allowed three chances to catch the Frisbee, and the best two of three would be counted.

I was amazed at the variety of dogs and owners participating. Many were border collies, but I also noticed other herding dogs: German shepherds, retrievers, and even a terrier.

The owners were just as varied: men and women, old and young, small and not so small, bold and shy. Some owners were nervous, but their dogs were calm. In other duets, the opposite was true. I had never seen such a mixture of dogs and people in one place.

Finally, Laura and I were at the head of the line. I stood calmly beside her as she set her grip on the Frisbee. I tensed as her arm came back, and she heaved the Frisbee into the air.

I charged immediately at top speed, my eyes not leaving the flying disk. Suddenly, I realized the Frisbee was not flying down the field but was heading toward the bleachers. What a terrible throw—the worst I had ever seen her make.

The Frisbee landed on the bottom row of spectator seats.

As I cautiously approached the area, a boy retrieved the Frisbee and handed it to me.

Even from this distance, I could see the disappointment on Laura's face. I carefully took the Frisbee from the boy and ran back to Laura.

Laura moved forward, and we met. She stooped down and told me how sorry she was for the bad throw. I knew that. She assured me that she would do better. I wagged my tail.

Laura stood in the same position she held before. She gripped the Frisbee firmly, glanced down at me, and threw. I rushed after the Frisbee, immediately delighted that she had thrown it right down the middle of the field at a good height and for a distance.

I charged after the Frisbee and then leaped into the air as it descended. I knew I had completed one of my most acrobatic jumps—and I caught the Frisbee.

The crowd cheered loudly. I was "dog of the day," at least for the moment. What a fantastic feeling! I proudly carried the Frisbee back to Laura and nodded to the crowd as I loped along. Laura's friends yelled and waved at me.

I dropped the Frisbee at Laura's feet. She picked it up, gave me a big hug, and motioned for me to get into position for the final throw. I was really excited. I danced around Laura as she got into position. This might be an even better attempt. She might throw it even farther.

Laura stood straight, set her feet, drew back her arm, and released the Frisbee.

I leaped after it. I couldn't believe what I was seeing. The Frisbee sailed toward the bleachers on the other side of the field.

I knew how badly the Frisbee had been thrown before I covered a few yards. I sensed Laura moving toward me. The Frisbee landed on the walkway in front of the bleachers.

I trotted over and picked it up, with Laura right behind me. People cheered as I held the Frisbee. The cheering helped, but my tail still dropped between my legs as I followed Laura around the bleachers and into the parking lot.

Laura knelt in front of me and told me how sorry she was that she'd made bad throws. She acknowledged that she had been more nervous than she'd thought she would be. I licked her hand. We had tried, and the shelter benefited. We would try again next year.

Border collies won both the distance and the style trophies.

Chapter 11

Saving Laura

The late-afternoon sun slid behind the backyard fence. I couldn't clearly see the Frisbee that Laura threw to me. The phone rang. Laura hurried into the house to answer it. When she finished the conversation, she called to me from the back steps.

"Come on, Shep, we need to get some more cash. I may have time to stop at a farmer's market after the breakfast meeting with our new state representative. I won't have time to stop in the morning."

I jumped into the car beside her. Laura didn't always buckle me into my harness if we were going only to the grocery store or to the ATM at her bank, and she didn't buckle me for this trip.

It was nearly dark before we arrived at the ATM. Laura parked in one of the small marked places close to the machine.

Laura leaned over and opened my window before she left the car. She trusted me not to jump out and knew I liked to investigate new smells wherever we stopped. I stuck my head out the window to see and smell everything.

Laura strolled to the ATM, retrieved her bank card from her wallet, and waited patiently while the man ahead of her took money from the machine. Laura moved to the ATM when the man left, slid her card into the machine, pushed a few buttons, and retrieved her cash.

A pickup truck with a company logo pulled in quietly beside our Subaru. I searched the face of the man in the driver's side and didn't like it—one of my dog-gut instincts.

I lay down so the man couldn't easily see me. I stuck my head over the bottom edge of the window and kept my eyes on him.

The man was dressed in black, including a black hood. He grabbed a long black bar from the passenger seat and stepped out of the truck.

The man grasped the bar firmly in his right hand and headed toward Laura, who was standing alone facing the machine as she counted her money. She turned around just in time to see the man lunge toward her.

"Shep, help me!"

I made a flying leap through the open window, charged the man, and threw my entire body high at the man's throat.

My speed, my weight, and my unexpected attack knocked the man off his feet. He fell hard, flat onto his back, and struck his head against jagged rocks surrounding the flower garden at the side of the ATM.

He struggled for a moment on the ground and then lay still. Blood seeped onto the rocks behind his head. The bar lay at his side.

A young couple responding to Laura's desperate shouts ran into the dimly lit space. The woman called the police.

Almost immediately, a police car with flashing emergency lights skidded to a stop behind our Subaru. Two officers jumped out, guns drawn. One approached Laura, and the other stood over the man on the ground.

Laura's voice quivered. "He tried to attack me—with that black bar. My dog saved me."

I rubbed my head against her leg.

While one officer examined the attacker, the couple offered more details.

"My wife and I were walking to the ATM from our apartment down the street. We saw the man creeping up to attack her. Sara called nine-one-one. We ran to help her. Out of nowhere, this black-and-white dog threw itself right at the man. The robber lost his balance and fell into the rocks."

His wife added, "We saw everything. The dog saved her."

The officer checking the suspect shook his head.

"We don't need the ambulance for this one."

Laura stood even closer to me. "My dog was protecting me. That man could have killed me."

"The guy was stupid to approach you when you had your dog with you," one of the officers said.

"I don't think he knew Shep was in my car. He was focused on robbing me."

Other police cars and an ambulance arrived. The officers gathered while the medical team examined the man.

"The suspect is dead. We'll have to take the dog with us," said an authoritative man in civilian clothes who introduced himself to Laura as Detective Simmons.

"No! My dog did nothing wrong. He saved my life." Laura grabbed my collar and hung on tight.

The first officer on the scene agreed.

"Detective, there's no indication that the dog did any more than knock down the suspect. The man fell hard into sharp rocks. That's not the dog's fault."

The detective continued to question Laura. She held tightly to my collar until someone brought her my leash. We were both directed toward one of the police cars. Laura and I sat in the back seat while Laura repeated her story. When she finished, the detective spoke.

"This ATM is the third one hit in this area in the last twenty-four hours. The suspect didn't wait until dark. Our officers arrived here so quickly because they were patrolling a few blocks from here. One woman was hospitalized as a result of an attack earlier this evening. A man was brutally attacked a few miles from that crime. Not many people paid attention to someone driving a company truck until it was too late."

A uniformed officer approached. "Ma'am, I've got to take your dog to the station. He's part of the crime scene. We'll need to do a few tests."

Laura refused to turn me over to the officer. She pleaded with him. I was proud of her. I didn't want to spend the night in a jail cell.

"Officer, I live only a few miles from here. Shep is not going anywhere but home. Let him stay with me. I'll bring him to you whenever his presence is required."

The detective interrupted. "I think we can allow them both to go home, under the circumstances. The dog did save its owner's life."

"And maybe the lives of others the suspect didn't get a chance to rob tonight," another officer added.

Laura tugged at my leash, and we climbed out of the detective's car. An officer approached her.

"OK, ma'am. You can take your dog home. We'll call you when we need him. We may need to take blood and other samples from his body."

Why would anyone want samples of my blood? Or anything else? Maybe I left a few hairs on the man's body—nothing more.

Laura and I drove home slowly. Tears ran down her cheeks.

I didn't know whether they were from relief or concern about me. I snuggled over and put my head into her lap, a move that was forbidden while she was driving. She smiled and stroked my head.

Neither one of us slept well that night.

Two days later, Laura and I were summoned to the police station. We were both nervous as we entered the building.

The officer at the reception desk asked Laura why she was bringing a dog into the police station.

"Because I was told to do so—by Detective Simmons."

"That's the dog? He doesn't look vicious to me."

"He's not a vicious dog," Laura snapped. "He was only protecting me."

Detective Simmons hurried our way.

"Come into my office, Laura, Shep."

Detective Simmons shuffled through papers on his desk.

"I have reports from the coroner's office. The suspect died at the scene from blunt-force head trauma caused by hitting his head against the rocks. No evidence that Shep bit him or even scratched him."

I could have written that report.

"Both of you are free to leave. I would like you to stop in the coffee room on your way out. Several people would like to congratulate Shep on his fine police work."

I was not eager to stop, even if Laura was pleased. We halted at the coffee room.

A reporter and photographer from the local paper intercepted us immediately. The photographer took several pictures of me. I wish I had been aware of what was my best side for a pose. I decided I liked being treated like a hero.

The reporter cornered Laura. She told him how we found each other at the animal shelter.

"Great story," the reporter said. "A shelter dog saves the person who saved him."

The attempted-robbery episode was not finished. Laura received a call the next week from the hospital where the woman who been attacked at another ATM was recovering. Laura and the woman chatted for a while. Laura nodded her head.

She finished her conversation, brushed me quickly, snapped on my leash, and led me to the Subaru. She fastened me into my harness, so I knew we were traveling farther than the grocery store or bank.

We drove to the same hospital where Laura had recovered from the wreck. Memories of those sad days were disturbing. I shook my head to clear such thoughts and wondered what we were doing there.

Laura let me out of the Subaru. Surely, she knew dogs were not allowed in the hospital.

As Laura and I headed toward the entrance, Trudy, the receptionist from the animal shelter, climbed out of a car on the other side of the parking lot. She carried a small terrier and waved to us.

We met her in front of the hospital.

"Hi, you two," Trudy said. She held the terrier out to us. "This is Crispy. Mrs. Warner, who was attacked at an ATM that horrible evening, called the shelter. She wanted two things: first, to meet Shep, and second, to adopt a dog from the shelter. The two of us decided that Crispy would be just the dog for her. Mrs. Warner is being discharged today and should be waiting at the door."

That was how my photo appeared in the paper a second time. Mrs. Warner held Crispy, and I sat on my haunches beside them.

Above the photo were the words, "Happy Ending for Robbery Victim and Shelter Dog." I felt great to be part of the story.

CHAPTER 12

Return to a Ranch

LAURA AND I had been together for several years. As a dog, I didn't keep track of time well, but winters had come and gone. I was contented, except on occasions when Laura insisted I go to the veterinarian for my annual checkup or to the dog wash.

Our elderly neighbor across the street moved out, and Kathy, a single woman about Laura's age, moved in along with Rusty, her German shepherd. Even though we were both males, we became friends. Laura and Kathy sometimes exchanged dog-sitting duties if either of them had to be gone overnight. Laura dragged an old bed of mine to Kathy's porch, and Rusty had a bed at my house.

I appreciated the arrangement. Although I enjoyed being boarded at the Barkleys for longer periods, I preferred to stay close to home for the overnights.

Laura accepted a job editing and proofreading for the state legislature while it was in session. She spent a lot of time at her computer and spent evenings and weekends at the state capitol. I wondered if she was always working at the statehouse.

Sometimes she wore skirts or dresses and heels to work.

One night, she came home late, humming and smiling to herself. She stretched out on the couch and called me to her side.

"Shep, you'll never guess what happened today. I ran into an old friend from college. Actually, he was more than a friend. His name is Phil Bower. We recognized each other, although it has been years since I've seen him. Neither one of us has changed much."

I could tell Laura was excited about seeing this man again. She seldom had much to say about any male—except for me, of course.

"And guess what, Shep. He and his wife are divorced. He raised his sons alone after she left him. He retired from an intelligence job with the military and has a small ranch in the mountains near Sweet Briar. I ran into him at a committee meeting where he was representing some sheep ranchers."

I cocked my head as I listened to Laura. This was more than a chance meeting of two old friends.

I was not surprised when Laura invited Phil to our home for a barbecue that weekend. She even let Phil grill the steaks.

Phil and I started sizing each other up the moment we met.

He was older than Laura, with gray at his temples, trim like she was, and I guess not bad looking for a human male.

Phil was curious about how I had come into Laura's life.

He said it was possible I had jumped or was thrown from a rancher's truck too far away from home to find my way back.

"You know, Laura," he said, "I'd say someone lost a valuable working dog. Maybe even a herding show dog. It certainly appears he was meant to be more than a pet."

Laura frowned, and I slapped my tail on the ground. What could be more important for me than to be Laura's dog and her to be my person?

The next time Phil visited, he brought Laura information that neither of us wanted to know. Phil explained that years ago a neighbor of his lost a valuable border collie he was training. Phil even brought a picture of the dog as a pup.

Laura gasped as she stared at the photo. Obviously, I was the pup in the photo. My unique white markings matched the pup's.

Laura agreed that I was probably the dog in the photo. Phil asked her what she planned to do about this revelation.

"Nothing, absolutely nothing," Laura said without hesitation. She shoved the photo back at Phil. That ended the conversation. I was relieved. Neither of them mentioned my former life when they were together, at least not when I joined them.

Laura and I drove to Phil's ranch to spend a weekend after the legislative session was over. When we arrived, Phil was talking with another rancher. Laura drove the Subaru to the men.

Laura tensed when the introductions were made. I leaned over Laura and glanced at the man, Keith Hardin, and quickly turned my head away from the window. Keith was my former owner. I wished I could escape, but all I could do was scrunch down in the seat.

Keith asked Laura if she would let Shep out of the car. She sensed I was uncomfortable. She stood by the door and clearly explained to Keith that I was her dog. She told him firmly that she had found me at the shelter and that she had no intention of giving me up.

Keith's face flushed. He insisted that he could undoubtedly identify me as his dog Lucas, who had been lost from his truck on the way to a herding competition.

Laura did not budge. "Shep was a stray—had been one for months. He was brought to the shelter injured and starving. He's my dog."

Phil acknowledged that he had invited Keith knowing that Laura and I were visiting.

In the past, Keith had often mentioned to Phil that he was distressed about losing one of his best competitors and even recently had said he would like to know what had happened to Lucas.

Laura wasn't listening. She was angry that Keith didn't care enough to contact the shelter in her area or place ads for the lost dog. Keith had no reason to think he had any claim on me. She cuttingly added that I would certainly be dead now if the rescuer hadn't taken me to the shelter.

What Laura did next surprised everyone. She opened the Subaru door and told Keith to call me. He shrugged and called, "Lucas, come here. Now."

I jumped out of the Subaru, ran around the car, and settled at Laura's feet. Keith again shouted at me. I ignored him.

Laura opened the driver's-side door. I jumped back into the Subaru.

Keith slapped the leg of his pants and strode toward his truck.

Laura's anger did not subside. She scooted me over and climbed into the Subaru, yelled good-bye to the men, and drove off.

Laura didn't stop until she reached the main road—and then only to buckle me into my harness.

I had never seen Laura so upset. She even took her eyes off the road. "Why did Phil do that? Was he thinking Keith really wanted his dog back? After all this time? Did he think I didn't care that much about you? Or maybe that I cared too much? Or was it he thought you'd be better off doing what you were born to do? I don't understand."

I carefully reached a paw in her direction. I didn't want to distract her driving any more than it already was.

Laura's voice choked, and she didn't say any more. I reached over as far as my harness would allow and licked her cheek—another no-no ordinarily. I heard her crying that night.

The next morning, I stayed close to Laura. I left her only for my food and water and to go outside. The phone rang several times during the day. Laura did not answer it.

A few days later, as I finished breakfast, Laura told me we were going camping. I wagged my tail. That sounded like fun. I watched as she put items into my backpack.

When Laura was satisfied with what she had packed for me and placed my backpack in the Subaru, she gathered her tent, sleeping bag, and the rest of her camping equipment. Last of all, she included her fishing pole. As soon as she finished packing the Subaru, Laura called me and held my harness in her hand. I ran toward her.

Laura's eyes had been red-rimmed the past few days. Today, they looked better, and she smiled a lot. She dressed in jeans, boots, and a sweatshirt. She even wore a little makeup. I jumped into the Subaru, and we were on our way.

We traveled for a couple of hours into the mountains near a lake. A state-park sign stood at the side of the road.

Laura drove past it and spoke to the ranger in a tiny booth at the park entrance. She had reserved a campsite.

We drove through the park until we found the campsite. I jumped out of the Subaru to investigate while Laura unloaded our things. I sniffed and sniffed. Many of these smells were not familiar to me, and I was eager to investigate further.

When I finished sniffing, I glanced around and noted that we had lots of company, even other dogs. I wagged my tail when Laura spoke to me. I wanted her to know how happy I was to be there.

Two teenagers ran over to our campsite. I stepped in between them and Laura, my usual position when I didn't know people. The boys offered to help Laura with the tent. I wasn't certain she wanted help and stood my ground. Laura leaned down and petted me.

"Shep, the boys are here to help."

When the boys raised the tent, I sniffed inside and outside of it. I had never been inside a tent on the ground before. It was much larger than our old truck tent.

Laura brought in a folded cot, my bed, and her sleeping bag. She finished setting up our campsite and said, "Shep, let's go to the lake."

Laura grabbed a small sack and headed down a path to the water. I followed for a few yards and then took my rightful place in front, leading the way.

The lake spread before us for as far as I could see. The opposite shore was a long distance from where we stood. As we strolled along the beach, Laura pulled a Frisbee from the sack. I scampered ahead of her. She threw the Frisbee. What a place to play! Laura soon threw the Frisbee into the lake intentionally, not too far from shore. I leaped into the water and joyfully swam to retrieve it.

I could have stayed at the lake until dark, but we left while there was still evening light. We hiked back to our campsite. Laura unwrapped the sandwiches she had brought and shared one with me after I ate my dog food.

Laura unfolded her new camp chair and sat down with cookies and a thermos of coffee. I listened to the voices of the campers around us. Someone played a guitar. What a wonderful place!

We finished our meal. Laura stepped inside the tent and lay down on the cot. She closed her eyes. I lay down on the ground beside her.

We must have slept for an hour or so. It was dark. I heard a strange noise outside and crept to the front of the tent. I stared at a curious animal sniffing around our tent. I met my first raccoon. I thought someone had struck the animal in both eyes. He slowly crept over to Laura's backpack, which was sitting in her camp chair. I barked, warning the critter to get out of our campsite. Laura stumbled out of the tent and laughed as she watched the raccoon amble away.

The first full day at the camp, Laura went fishing and hooked a trout. I watched, fascinated, as she worked the line. When she reeled in the trout, it flopped at my feet on the sandy beach. I waited while she cleaned the fish. Later, she cooked it over the campfire. We shared the meal. Trout tasted almost as good as ice cream.

A small general store was located about a mile from our campsite. Laura and I hiked over each day with the backpack and Frisbee. I became quite the attraction. I was not the only dog around, but I was the only one who would chase and catch Frisbees. Kids loved to throw the Frisbee for me. One afternoon, I played so long that I actually became tired, really tired of chasing that round disk.

Laura and I spent two wonderful days at the state park. Each evening, Laura built a campfire for us. I enjoyed its warmth as the night became chilly. The park could be my second home as far as I was concerned.

Early in the morning of our last day at the campsite, Laura sat contentedly with her coffee while enjoying the scenery and the brisk air. I lay next to the fire she had built.

A green truck roared up the road leading to our campsite.

I recognized the vehicle as Phil's. Laura noticed the truck approaching and stood up quickly. I barked. Phil did not belong there.

Laura showed surprise at seeing Phil. He climbed out of his truck and marched over to her. I took my usual position between Laura and the approaching person. Laura quietly spoke my name, and I lay down at her feet.

"What are you doing here?" Laura asked Phil.

"I had to find you to apologize about Shep," Phil said. "I thought I was doing the right thing—bringing Shep and Keith together again. I was wrong. I stupidly thought Shep might be happier as a working sheep dog. I'm so sorry."

"How did you know I was here?"

"Well, you hadn't answered either of your phones for days. I got worried and drove to your home. You and Shep were both gone, of course. I remembered you once said you liked to go camping. I decided you were somewhere with Shep, so I called a friend with the forest service and found out you were here. The ranger pointed out your campsite. I thought I'd drop by for a cup of coffee, if you'd share one with me."

Laura grinned. "You came a long way for a cup of coffee."

Laura stepped up and hugged Phil briefly.

"I really don't understand why you thought Shep would be happier as a working dog. Shep and I are a package deal."

"I may not have understood that before, but I certainly do now. Will you two give me a second chance?"

"I've always believed in second chances," Laura said. "Have some coffee."

I decided to snoop around the back of the campsite because people acted silly sometimes.

I finished my snooping and moved back to where Phil and Laura were standing. A little while later, the two of them packed up the camping equipment.

"Shep, Phil has invited us back to his ranch. Want to give him a second chance?"

I hesitated. I wasn't sure about Phil.

Phil tried to encourage me. "You'd have the entire ranch to explore. And I can throw a Frisbee farther than Laura."

I glanced up at him and offered my paw.

He leaned down and took it.

"Shep, I learned that I never should have thought about you wanting to be somewhere without Laura. Men can learn. OK?"

I let him shake my paw.

The next weekend, we drove down the dirt road to Phil's ranch. I noticed sheep grazing in a pasture. Would I someday show them who was boss? Maybe.

THE END